I WANT IT TO HAPPEN

I Want It to Happen

Love as a Saga

A Novel by Samuel Hazo

PITTSBURGH:
Serif Press, 2022

Cover design by Jason Price.

Serif Press
SerifPress.com

For Diane

"I cannot say I loved, for who can say
He was killed yesterday?"

—*John Donne*

TO HIM it was not a sunset but a decrescendo. Others saw the world in images. Tonio saw it as music. The sound of a horse's hooves in full gallop came to him in triplets. Thunder was a bursting bang of cymbals. A traffic snarl with all horns blasting made him think of an orchestra tuning up. The steady drops of lengthening pods of water from a faulty tap in the cellar were like whole notes—one, one, one, one. The pauses between the drops were whole rests.

"Are you going to show me what you're writing in that journal, Lue?"

"Only when it's perfect, and even then I don't know, Tonio."

"You're faithful to it."

"I have to be, honey. It helps me."

"Then I won't ask any more."

He leaned across to her and kissed her on the cheek. She purred, liking it.

"That tastes like more," she said. She looked up at him and smiled. When he straightened up again, she said, "You're losing your hair, Tonio. See what marrying me did to you."

"It's all in the genes. If hair was a recessive in a great grandfather way far back, it's easy to see why it's a recessive in me. You had nothing to do with it. Blame it on my abuelo."

"Would it make you feel good if I told you I like the way you look now better? Some men look better when they start to lose their hair, and you're one of them."

"Come on. That doesn't matter to me anymore. It used to, but not anymore." He smiled at her. "Besides, you're heard the old story. Baldness is supposed to be a sign of excessive virility. That's magazine language. I'm just quoting."

"I wish we could test that theory."

"We'll have time. Hold your horses."

She returned his smile and eased herself closer to him. He was seated in blue pajamas on one side of the sofa, and she was lying on her back on the rest of the sofa with her head resting on his thigh. She held his left hand in her right and began touching his fingertips in sequence with her thumb, counting them over and over.

"I just counted to ten on your fingertips," she said.

"In English or Spanish?"

"In English. I always count in English."

"Spanish is better for praying, more musical. You could say your beads in Spanish. Your Spanish is as good as mine, Lue."

"Where did I read that you always pray in your first language."

"Is that right? It sounds right."

"People don't say the rosary much anymore. It's part of the old Catholic religion."

"Rosaria's daughter does. Her mother told me that today."

"How is she?"

"She forgives him. What else can I say?"

"I'd never forgive him for that."

"But she does. And she was the victim."

"I don't even want to think about it."

"It's hard not to think about it, but if the girl feels that way about it, who are we to say anything?" He held her hand tightly in his. "Look out there." The dusk was making the western sky a sequence of purples and oranges and reds and blues. The sun seemed to be balanced on the very plane of the horizon like a russet billiard ball on a tabletop. "Take a look at the first and only sunset on the final Thursday of July in the year of Our Lord 1990. If you miss it, you miss it forever. No repeat."

HOW MANY people do you know who have a church-word for a first name? Not many, I'll bet. For years I hated it, hated the sound of it. Halley-looooo-ya Quinn. It sounded like the name of some revival meeting or ... Hell, I don't know what it sounded like, but I was stuck with it. It actually took me years to stop hating it. And then, you know what happened? Go ahead, guess. I'll bet you'll never ... I started to like it for the same reason I hated it in the first place. It was different. It made me feel different, and I like feeling different. Girls are like that. Women are like that. We all want to be the one and only no matter what we're the one and only of, right?

I don't know what I'm writing this for, Carolina. Maybe it's just to keep myself busy. I don't know if I'll ever let you see this notebook, but I have to have someone to write to, or my pen won't budge. What else can I say? You've come through all this with me. We're just like sisters, closer than sisters. Of course, I never had a sister—or a brother, for that matter—so how would I know? But I can imagine, can't I? Isn't writing wonderful? I sit here watching the words come out of the end of my pen, letter by letter. They're just scratches, but we all agree that the scratches mean what we want to say. Isn't that something to think about? I'm making American scratches. Someone in China is making Chinese scratches right now, I'll bet. If you were writing to your mother, you'd be making Spanish scratches. And they all mean something. Where would we be without them?

The real trouble in my family started with my Dad. He was the one who picked my name for me, by the way. For some reason he thought that Halleluiah was the most beautiful word he ever heard. He used to say that every syllable could stand by itself. Hall-ley-lu-iah. And that's how he used to say it—four syllables like four whole notes in music, four beats of the drum. You figure that out.

Anyway, my Dad was at sea most of the time. So Muz and I would be by ourselves for months on end. That's the way the Navy was in those days.

Maybe it still is. I don't know. I don't keep up with stuff like that. The military gives me a pain you know where. I don't like anything where everybody looks the same. But getting back to my Dad—he was a petty officer on a destroyer up until I was in my teens, and his ship was never in port. If you joined the Navy then to see the sea, you sure as hell saw the sea. Months at a time. Once he was gone for almost a whole year.

But it wasn't just his being away. He didn't stay in touch. I mean he wasn't the kind of man who wrote letters, and that was rough on Muz. It got to her. There were times she took out her disappointment and loneliness on me, over-scolding me for some little thing I did or flaring up over nothing at all or crying her eyes out when she thought I couldn't see her do it and then getting mad at me because I caught her at it. It's tough enough being a woman, but being a lonely woman and trying to hide it is the toughest thing of all.

Even during those times when my Dad was ashore (that was his word for it—he was either at sea or ashore), he was still really at sea on that damn ship. I mean he was so used to being with a lot of men all the time that he really didn't understand us—females, that is. Muz was the loser both ways—when he was home or when he was away. One time late at night I heard them arguing. I couldn't make out what the argument was about, but my Dad was all worked up, and he was using that word every other word. I could hear Muz crying. Then I think I heard him hit her or something like that. And then there were sounds that two people make when they're, you know, together. I mean, doing it. And then there was more silence, and finally Muz said right out loud plain as anything, "Before, you curse me and hit me, and, afterword, you don't say a word for me. I deserve more than that, Frank. I'm not just a receptacle, you know. I'm not going to let you treat me like one, not any more."

Well, that was the beginning of the end for them, and they both knew it. I don't blame Muz for drinking more than she should have after that. What else was there for her? She didn't believe in cheating. All she wanted in life was to love one man, and my Dad turned out to be the wrong man. It happens.

Carolina, while I'm writing this, the most beautiful little yellow and black bird came and landed on the windowsill. He's looking right at me. Now he's hopping around and pecking at the window. Isn't that funny. Somehow that seems so important and interesting to me, and last year at this time I wouldn't have noticed it, or, if I did, I'd probably have tried to shoo him away. Now I look at him like company. Honest. I'll miss him when he flies away. I really will. Does that make sense?

If my Dad didn't have much love for Muz, he had a hell of a lot less for me. And I felt it. By the time I got to be a teenager, I was a pushover for any guy who'd pay attention to me. I mean I'd fall in love in a minute just for a kind word—a kind, male word. It touched something in me. Sometimes I was so lonely that I was tempted to go all the way with some guy. You know, just thinking what the hell... But I always caught myself in time. I guess the psychologists can tell you why a girl with my kind of a father and a mother who drank on the side and cried into her pillow every night would be more or less starved for affection. They probably even have a word for it. They have a word for everything, those guys. All I knew then and all I know now is that I had something hollow inside of me the size of the Grand Canyon, and there were a lot of boys my age and older who sensed it, and I was ready and waiting for them. It was just their attention I wanted at first, mind you. As soon as one of them got fresh or tried something with his hand under my dress or anything like that, I'd give him a good smack. I gave out a lot of smacks, and sometimes I even had to fight my way out of those clinches. But I have myself to blame. Sooner or later a guy's gonna make a move like that because that's what they do, right? It's in the genes. At some point they just have to do something like that.

As for my looks, well, I was shaping up all right if you don't mind my saying so. That's really a terrific time in a girl's life, Carolina. It's when you feel yourself turning into something really female. You start to enjoy looking at yourself. You start to fill out. My legs were just starting to get some shape to them, and I was doing all right in other places, too. You know, upstairs. If I put my mind to it, I could get a man—any man—to look at me. It's not that hard, really. Even the dumbest girl knows how to do that. And all the time in the background there was Muz warning me about fast boys and all the rest, but I let it go in one ear and out the other. I was having too much fun, and I was starting to get so damn good-looking I couldn't stand it. It was also about that time that Muz and my Dad split up for keeps. The split didn't change things much. They were split long before they split, if you know what I mean. But the actual split took hope out of the picture. Muz just stopped looking for my Dad to change some day in the future. She always kept a little hope alive up to that point. But after the split, not a flicker.

By that time I was nineteen, and I was still carrying around that big hollowness inside of me. You know how girls get, Carolina, when they just want somebody to love, or rather someone to love them. If you let it get to you, it's always on your mind. That's the way I was. And just about then I met Fred. He had shoulders that really filled out a shirt, and he could dance like Fred Astaire. I don't know to this minute if it was the shoulders or the dancing that made me go ga-ga, but that's the way I went. On second thought, I think it was the dancing because I love to dance, and Fred had a built-in sense of rhythm, and he knew all the steps and then some. Anyway, when Fred danced with me, I felt like I was made out of balloons. Of course, that was my usual reaction. Any time I ever got tight with a guy before Fred and, of course, including Fred, I felt that I was lighter than air. Then reality would set in, and then I had to live with the fallout and the heartache and all the rest of the romantic hangover. I mean, until I met Tonio. But then Tonio is one in a zillion. Make that a quadruple zillion. And you can believe me when I tell you that because I ought to know. I know you knew him before I did, but he's done things for me that no man would ever do for any woman, and he makes it seem like no big deal. But that's getting ahead of the story.

But when I was just this side of twenty, what in the name of oranges did I know about love? Or about men, for that matter? If it had pants on and was halfway interesting and polite and reasonably good-looking, I was on-your-mark-get-set-and-go interested. But looking back on it, I think the first time I got serious with any one of them was when I met Fred. And God, was I wrong. I was emotionally wrong, morally wrong, intellectually wrong, historically wrong, and, well, just plain wrong, but who knows that in advance, right? For a while I was serious enough to go with the feeling, which is the worst thing you can do. Those dance-steps of his made me fall in a big way, and I thought everything was going to be like Snow White and the Prince. Famous last words, right? Right. After half a month he wanted me to go to bed with him. He said it would be just like dancing, waist to waist, all that stuff. And he kept at it, making it sound better and better and more delicious all the time. No rough stuff, just talk. He told me that most people just looked at it nowadays like shaking hands. He said he would take precautions, not to worry. Everybody was doing it. Well, it never happened. Thank God for small favors. When Muz saw how smitten and confused I was, she told me to give Fred up or leave the house. She said I couldn't play both ends against the middle—not in her house I couldn't. Of course, she was dead right. But I was smitten, smatten, smutten. I thought I had to prove something. I was twenty and so damn sure that I knew everything there was to know that I actually moved out. Miss Independence. For one night. I went to Fred's. But when I told him the situation and that I wanted to stay, he just backed off. He really pulled out of it. And that showed me that it was just biology between us. No love at all. I fooled myself into thinking that I loved him, but that night I saw that he just wanted me. Not the me on the inside that needed the real thing, but just the female parts of me. Frankly, we were both thinking with our glands. That's what sex does to you sometimes. It just takes over, and it makes you think that you're really thinking, but you're not. That incident with Fred should have told me something about myself, but it didn't. Or maybe it did, and I wasn't listening hard enough.

Don't you wonder, Carolina, what draws two people to one another? I've read so many stories about it. There's an old story somewhere that men and women really started out as one creature, and then the creature was split into male and female, and ever since then each of us is incomplete. But finding just any old male doesn't make up for it. It has to be one particular one. Last month I read in a magazine that your body knows the one for you before your mind does. And I think I believe it. Your body just waits for your mind to catch up with it. It may take months or even years, but the body won't change. It knows. It knew all along. If you ask me, the whole thing is a mystery. There are all these tests these days about how opposites attract and how everything's in the stars anyway, so why fight it? But that's a cop-out. It's deeper than that. I'm not saying I understand it, but I respect the mystery in it. Maybe we're not supposed to understand. Maybe it's beyond us. What do you think?

Anyway, I went back home early the next morning. Fred and I had stayed up and talked all night. He felt as long as he was talking, he'd keep me at arm's length. He sure as hell didn't want me to move in, that's for sure. Muz took me back without a word, and we had a big cry over it—actually more than one cry—and I went out and got a job and took up my college work where I left off. Deep down I was still the same old pushover, the same old romantic, still looking forward to the next big experience but not really learning from the experiences I'd already had. Is that romantic, or is that romantic?

I'm thinking now, Carolina, how lucky I was that I never went out with anybody really dangerous. Look at what happened to Rosaria's daughter. She agreed to go out with some guy to the senior prom as a stand-in for a friend because the friend had mono. She didn't think twice about it. She was just doing somebody a favor. Well, this kid started to get physical with her on the way home, and she fought him. And he pulled a knife on her and raped her and then stabbed her eight times and dumped her on the side of the road. It was eight hours before they found her. She thought she was dead, but someone found a pulse, and they worked on her and worked on her and brought her back. That was three weeks ago. Now they tell me that she's coming along all right. Doesn't remember a thing about what happened to her, thank God. Doesn't remember all of it, I mean. She remembers the kid and how he raped her, but after the first stab, it's all a blank. That kid's in jail now. He was hiding in the basement when they came to his house to arrest him. His mother went hysterical. She wouldn't believe it. She fought the police like a tiger. Rosaria's daughter's amazing. She's one of those charismatics or whatever they call themselves. She refuses to hate the guy. She told her mother, "Mom, I'm glad it was me and not someone else who couldn't handle something like this." Can you imagine a girl having an attitude like that? It's not naive or anything like that. She really believes every word she says. I couldn't say that on a bet. I'd strangle the bastard with my bare hands. And I'd do it slow, honestly. I know it's not the Christian way to feel, but that's how I would feel, Christianity or no Christianity.

After that business with Fred, I buried myself in schoolwork. I didn't know what I wanted to be, so I was interested in everything: history, literature, philosophy, art, language. I studied Spanish for three and a half years. A beautiful language, Carolina. And I'm not telling you this just because you're Spanish. Speaking Spanish always makes me feel like I'm speaking music. And, of course, it really helped me a lot later when I met Tonio. Especially with his father.

I stayed romantic. I tried to correct myself, honestly. The only trouble was that I couldn't keep my heart in line. I was always falling in and out of love with some Thomas, Richard or Harold, and every time it started out to be something permanent. Every single damn one started out with that kind of promise. Then something would happen, and I'd wake up—too late as always, and I'd learn that I'd been kidding myself from the start. The healing process would start, and after a few months I'd be myself again, but it seems I never really learned. Don't misunderstand. I tried to learn each time why and how and where things went wrong, but the lesson never sank in. I don't know why. Let's just say I was a soft touch where romance was involved and that I wasn't exactly lucky in love up to that point and that I was the slowest learner on this earth. But that was all pre-Tonio. Without Tonio I never would have learned a thing

The first time I met Tonio was in the cafeteria at the college when I spilled a glass of iced tea on him. Accidentally, of course. I was heading for a table just before my Spanish class and lost my grip on my tray just as I was passing the table where he was sitting. The iced tea went all over his shoulder, and three ice cubes landed in his salad. He jumped a foot. He hadn't seen it coming, and the iced tea was cold. Well, you can imagine how embarrassed I was.

But after he cleaned himself up a bit and after we both got over the surprise of the whole thing, he was a really good sport about it. He even asked me to sit down with him, and I said why not, and I did sit down. And then we talked. That's how it was the first time, Carolina.

Now let me tell you up front that I didn't feel a thing then for Tonio. He just wasn't my type, whatever that means. You know that Tonio's not bad looking, not by a long shot, but he didn't have the kind of looks I'd always had in mind. He didn't fit the pattern.

Anyway, we just sat and talked, and I noticed that his shirt was not getting any drier. When I told him that, he just shrugged and said he couldn't very well go to class with a wet shirt. He smiled when he said that. That was his first smile in front of me, and it made his whole face happy. I liked it. I mean I like it when people smile or laugh completely. I see so many people who smile like Nixon. The smile has no connection to the rest of them. I can't stand that. It's the same as lying, isn't it?

After I saw that smile, I decided to cut my Spanish class, and we stayed right there in the cafeteria and talked until the place closed. To be honest with you, I have to say that I did most of the talking. In fact, to be really honest, I did just about all of the talking. You've probably noticed that I'm quite a talker. And I write just like I talk, so you can get an idea from what I'm writing now about the real me. But by then you'll know me by now better than I know myself, so what the hell. Anyway, I did most or rather all of the talking that night. I couldn't seem to help it. Actually, it's just the way I am, the way I've always been. Whatever I'm thinking I have to say straight out just to show myself that I'm really thinking it. It's like checking yourself in the mirror to make sure you are who you are. Talking is just like a mirror for me. I have to hear myself say what I'm thinking. Tonio listened to everything I said. He really listened, looking me straight in the eyes all the time.

He has those dark brown Mexican eyes, and they look straight through you. X-ray eyes I call them.

They make you feel that you have no defenses left, not a single one, I swear. I liked the way they made me feel. They actually put me in touch with myself, if you know what I mean. Maybe it was because I felt that I had Tonio's complete attention. Of course, I know now that that's the kind of attention he gives to everything, but I didn't know that then. It was a new experience for me, having someone listening only to me, just me. Most of the time when I talk to people, they're looking over my shoulder like they're searching for somebody they'll be talking to next. But not Tonio. He looks at you like you're the only person left in the whole universe, and actually he makes you feel that you are. His father has that same way of looking at you, but that's getting ahead of the story because I didn't meet his father until a month later...

Getting back to that night of our first talk in the cafeteria ... Tonio kept listening to me the whole time the way a doctor listens to your heartbeat, that closely, not missing a murmur. I kept waiting for him to pick up, to say something, but mostly he just smiled that smile of his. So, on I went. Then, when he finally did say something, he stopped me right in my tracks. He just said, "I get the impression that you're looking for something, but you don't know what it is."

Well, that stopped me cold. I even felt a little insulted, and I was ready to tell him so when I realized that what he said was the truth. So, I just sat there like a damn fool, and I didn't say a thing because I couldn't. And still he kept those brown eyes on me, and there was so much truth in them that I couldn't look into them for long before I had to look away. They were the most honest eyes. It was like looking into, say, a dog's eyes. I don't mean that as an insult or anything. I mean it as a compliment. Have you ever tried to stare back at a dog when he's looking at you? He doesn't blink. He just looks as straight as his eyes can look, and there's nothing but the truth in them, and after a while you just have to look away because with him it's not a game. He's absolutely sincere. Well, Tonio looks at everyone that way.

Let me stop here for a minute and tell you more about Tonio. I mean about my Tonio. You knew him before I did, and some of what I'm going to say you already know, but I have to get it down. You remember what I just said about how I need to talk to know what I know. Well, the same thing applies to writing. So here goes.

Tonio's not what you would call a handsome man. I mean he doesn't have the kind of looks they feature in the States. Marlboro man, Robert Redford, that kind of looks. Tonio's Mexican, and he looks Mexican. You might call him a man's man. He has a man's looks, a working man's looks. There's no other way to describe him. But after you get used to his looks, he makes all the other men you know look like boys. That's the only way to put it. All that work he did in the fields when he was a boy in Texas before the family came to Los Angeles left him strong, work-strong. And that's not the same as sports-strong. Tonio has work muscles. I mean he has the kind of permanent muscles that only hard work can create. And he has something else too. He has dignity. Plain simple human dignity. You notice it when he's standing alone or when he's with other people or when he's with his students. He's definite. He's all there just as himself. You look at those shoulders and those heavy eyebrows over those x-ray brown eyes and then at that straight strong nose and those flat Indian cheeks that cut away to his I-dare-you chin, and you know you're in the presence.

I learned later that his students were always a little afraid of him, and Tonio told me that that's the way it's supposed to be. He said that someone in charge always had to create a little fear in those he was in charge of. It's not in anything you do. It's how you're put together, how you make them feel. They have to know that they can go only so far, and that's it or else. Tonio's not mean to them or anything. He's just the kind of man who looks a little mean when he's thinking. And Tonio's always thinking. And thinking automatically makes him frown, and frowning makes him look like he's mad at somebody, and that translates into mean for a lot of people who don't know the real Tonio.

Now let me jump ahead to the next time I saw Tonio after I spilled iced tea on him in the cafeteria. It was in the cafeteria again. He was sitting exactly where he was sitting when I saw him the first time, and I accidentally on purpose went right up to him. Surprise, surprise. He stood up and held my chair for me. Would you believe that he was the first man who ever did that for me? And that impresses me. I don't care how much women want to be equal these days, but I sure as hell am one woman who comes to a dead stop when I run into a guy with manners, let me tell you.

I have this friend, Carolina, who's always arguing with her husband about women's rights and all that. She's very militant about it. I am too, to be honest with you, but I'm no Nazi. I mean I don't think that men are just there to fertilize us and that's all. There are two sexes, after all. Two. Anyway, this friend of mine got all worked up one day and said to her husband, "All we want is equality.

Absolute equality." And you know what her husband tells her? "It's a long way down."

Back to that second meeting in the cafeteria. We talked for a little while. You know, just chit chat. And then we went to class, me to Spanish 301, and Tonio to a class in music theory. Did I ever tell you that Tonio was voted one of the best band directors in all Los Angeles? I'm sure Tonio never said a word about it, but I can do it for him. Did you know about that? He's the bestest of the best. Well, just before we split to go to class, he asked me if he could drive me home. And I said sure, why not, I'd like that. So, we met where he asked me to meet him in the parking lot, and he opened the door of his ten-year-old Camaro for me the same way that he'd helped me with my chair in the cafeteria, and off we went. Neither of us said much for a few miles, and in the silence between us I thought again of how he told me he thought I didn't know what I was looking for in life, and, sitting there and watching Tonio drive, I realized that he didn't tell me that to insult me or offend me (even though it did). He was just putting his finger on the weak spot in my life, and he was straight enough to tell me so and then leave it go at that.

I'd never met a man like Tonio before. Anyone that truthful. Most of the guys I knew would hand you a line, or else they'd start to needle you until they started an argument instead of the conversation they were trying to start or else they flattered you with a lot of bull because they wanted something from you. I don't have to draw you a picture. I'm sure you've seen your share too. But Tonio didn't fit into any of that stuff. He was just himself. Just Tonio.

After we drove a few miles, Tonio puts some terrific cassette of Mexican music on the car stereo, and, I swear to God, I thought we were in Monterey or Vera Cruz or some place like that. It wasn't the usual Mexican stuff that they play for tourists—"La Cucaracha" and the rest. This was slower and more serious. Toni asked me then if I liked music and I said I liked this kind of music because my taste runs to ballads and classical. I told him I liked Vivaldi and opera, except German opera, which makes me feel older and more tired than I like to feel. But give me an Italian opera, and I'm in heaven on roller skates. You can sit back and swim in that music and have a good cry because it's all so romantic and beautiful. I never get enough of it. Tonio just listened, and he didn't say anything for the longest time, and the Mexican music kept filling up and filling up that little Camaro. Then he said something that nobody else ever said to me, and he said it in the same way he told me that I was looking for something in my life but didn't know what it was. He said, "You respond to the right things in music, and that's good. And you know what you like, and that's better. And you listen with your whole life, not just with your ears, and that's the best of all." That made me feel terrific. I thanked him for that, but I said he was probably over-rating me because I didn't really know much about music technically. I just knew what I liked, and I let myself like it no matter what anybody else said about it. He smiled that half-smile of his and said, "You don't know how rare that is. Most people aren't even confident enough to let themselves like what they really like. They like what somebody tells them to like. They follow somebody else's taste, and so they never really develop a taste of their own. You're different."

Just then we turned off the freeway to my neighborhood, and I guided him to the house. I was still thinking about what he said. He saw me to the door, and I introduced him to Muz. He smiled again when he said good-night, and then he left, and that was that.

Three days later I received a dozen of the reddest roses I ever saw in my life. And on the card was this note, "If what you're looking for in your life is roses, here they are." And the signature was just a capital T. Well, how do you respond to something like that? You just sit back and appreciate it. It was a first for me.

A week later Tonio asked me if I wanted to go with him to a flower show. A flower show! Now how could I say no to that even if I wanted to, and, frankly, I didn't want to. And I'm glad I went because it showed me a different side of Tonio. Don't misunderstand me. I always knew there was more to Tonio than met the eye, but I couldn't put my finger on what it was. He was really sensitive. I mean he was sensitive the way an artist is sensitive when he's trying to mix colors to find the right color or the way a surgeon is sensitive with an incision or the way a mother is sensitive with her own baby. You know, Carolina. Sensitive.

He gave me a real flower tour. He knew the names of every flower in the place in three languages. English, Spanish and Latin. Latin! How many men do you know who can say that? And he told me which flowers did better in sunlight and which did better in the shade. and he told me which ones bloom in which months during the summer. And a lot more. I asked him where he learned all this. And why. He just said he loved flowers because all they wanted in life was to be beautiful. That's all. And then he said, "Each flower is like a flag of its own little country. It's just out there in the sunlight living off its roots and trying to be the best and only thing it can be. It's not in competition with any other flower. It just believes in bloom-and-let-bloom so that every flower has a chance to be beautiful in its own place at its own time. And then it blends with all the other flowers that are out there doing the same thing. It's just like the orchestras and bands that I work with at school. I try to get each player to do his or her best. I say they might not be able to appreciate the total effect because they're just one small part of the whole orchestra—one flower in the field. But I tell them that every contribution counts and that the total sound and the total effect is the sum of a lot of individual contributions." And then he just went on about the way a lot of girls are named after flowers in Spanish—and in English too—because girls and flowers had that wish in common to be beautiful. He talked more than I expected, and it wasn't just chatter. He was talking from his soul, and I listened to every word.

I kept telling myself how unique Tonio was. Here I was with a man who was more than six feet high, was not the kind of man that anyone could push around, had arms like a wrestler's and was talking to me about some of the most delicate things in this world. I mean to tell you I was impressed. It wasn't a case of being overwhelmed, you understand, or falling in love the way I usually did, which means all the way with no thinking until later. This was different. This was someone who was being intimate with my mind. He was sharing something with me just for the sake of sharing it. No ulterior motive. No angle. No gimmick. Nothing at all like that.

I looked at him a few times just to see if this was on the level or just a new line. But it was the real thing. That's the one thing that's been true about Tonio Vargas from the first day I met him. He says straight out just what he feels and thinks. Otherwise, he doesn't say a thing. How many people do you know like that? How many men do you know like that?

SHE followed his hands as he spoke. He had a habit of using his hands almost as a form of speech, and she knew it was not simply a consequence of his being Mexican but of his being a drummer. She had heard that drummers as a group never could sit still or talk without using their hands.

"I tell them that music is like fire, Lue. It's something anybody can make. The neighborhood where I work is one of the worst. Drugs, theft, everything. When I started, they tried everything on me to see how much they could get away with. Once I picked up one kid and actually body-slammed him because he gave me the finger. And then I thought—I'm here to educate these kids, not defeat them. So, I left a little room for peace. But I worked them as hard as I could. I told them that I'd make them the best if they worked with me.

"I've always thought that music has to be a big part of high school education. It cuts across everything—science, commerce, math. Everybody responds to music, and it's an alternative to all the violence and ugliness that these kids see every day. And it's helped to save a lot of them.

"My favorites are the drummers. Guess why. The Bible says in the beginning was the word, but I say in the beginning was the drum. When I'm building a band in school, I build it around the drummer. The drummer's the pulse, the heartbeat. That's all a drummer does really, imitate the beat of the heart. He can vary the beat any time he wants, but the basic beat is the heartbeat.

"It doesn't matter how sophisticated we've gotten about drums, it starts and ends with that link between music and life. And that goes for dance too, especially dances done to drum-rhythms. In Africa the drum and the dance are like man and wife. What's between them is sacred. I read somewhere that one African dancer went into a fit—almost like someone with epilepsy—because the drummer varied the drumbeat just one iota when he wasn't supposed to. He was monkeying around with the rhythm of life, and the dancer went haywire because of it.

"You can't underestimate the link between rhythm and life, Lue. If you want to soothe a baby, rock him to a rhythm. Play patty cake. It's all a rhythm. It all leads back to the heartbeat and the drum. The beat is a natural attention-getter. You can't ignore it. If I start tapping my finger on a table to a regular beat, sooner or later it will get your total attention. You can't resist it. You could tune out an explosion or a lot of clatter, but on balance I'll bet no one could resist a steady tapping of my finger on the top of a table.

"I even use the drum as therapy when I teach. I try to find my most aggressive kids and get them started on the drum. They start to work out their aggressions when they play—some of them anyway. Not many of them go on to be interesting drummers, but so what? It tames them for a while or even permanently, and that's what education should do. Make people better than they are. Not everybody can play like Krupa or Rich or the great ones. But everybody has a sense of rhythm, and that rhythm comes right out of the beat of the heart."

Halleluiah loved to hear Tonio talk about music. His eyes took on a luminosity that gave them a life of their own and the words came as if he didn't have to think about them. At those times she studied his face as if she wanted to memorize forever the exact way he looked as he spoke.

THE next time I saw Tonio was almost the last time. The last time for me, I mean. He insulted me. Well, he really didn't insult me as much as he embarrassed me. Actually, it was a blessing in disguise, but I didn't realize it at the time. It happened at a dance. Who took me? No, not Tonio. It was, you guessed it, Fred. I hadn't seen him for more than two years. One night he called right out of the wild blue yonder and said there was a dance at one of the country clubs he went to and would I like to go? Old romantic me. Just when I heard his voice, my heart started to beat faster, and, even though I thought of seven-times-seven reasons why I should have told him then and there where he could shove his old dance, I heard myself saying okay as if nothing in the world had ever gone wrong between us.

After I hung up, I couldn't believe what I'd said. I had the idea of calling him right back and nixing everything, but I didn't even have his number, so what the hell. Then I wondered how or if I was going to tell Muz. But I did tell her in the end, straight out as if I was doing something brave. Muz just shook her head and told me just as straight, "The first time with him was a mistake, and that was forgivable because you weren't even twenty-one. This time it's a sin."

Sin or no sin, I let Fred take me to the dance. He came in this white Cadillac convertible, and off we flew. He told me that he was an agent for a rock band and that he had more money than he could spend. That, I suppose, was his way of explaining the Cadillac, but I let it pass. To this day I don't know if he was telling me the truth or not. The car had zebra leather on the seats, and the whole interior smelled of enough cologne to last into the middle of next week. Or maybe it was shaving lotion. Something like that. It smelled like a mixture of leather and spice. You fill in the blanks. And Fred had one of those quick tans you can get from a sun lamp or that bronzing paste that comes in a tube. He was wearing a white sport coat with a yellow silk shirt open at the collar, and he had a neck chain with what he told me was a 24-karat replica of a South American hot pepper on it. Said it was for good luck. But what did I know? Besides, I've always had a thing about jewelry. Rings, necklaces, earrings, they all give me a pain. Everything has to be coordinated, and one earring's always getting itself lost, so what the hell.

Anyway, back to the story. Here's Fred, all spiffed up in this convertible with the jungle decor, and there I am beside him wondering why I agreed to go out with him in the first place. After all, what did I owe him? He used me, and then he dumped me. I've read stories where people kill people for less than that. But I just let it pass. Maybe I'm too forgiving, or maybe I have the kind of memory that blots out the bad things. I've never decided what made me go, but if ever there was a turning point in my life, that was when it happened. That dance. That night.

So, we finally arrive at this club way up on top of a hill with sidelights in the driveway to the front door and valet parking and all the rest. The place is packed. People are dancing on top of one another, and the music is so loud you can feel it in your bones.

While I'm on the subject of music, Carolina, what about all this electric music? I mean medically speaking. What kind of people are we going to be sooner or later (and maybe sooner) if we can't hear one another because we've had too many blasts, and the eardrums can't take it?

No more social philosophizing. Back to the dance at the club. I don't know a soul there. Fred introduces me to two of his buddies and their dates. I notice that his buddies have the same neck chains on with the same gold peppers on them, and I figure it's a sign of something, but I don't know what, and I care less. And the two dates have on tights that fit them like a surgeon's glove. I mean you can see the works—crease, hump and all. No skirts. I remember asking myself why did they wear anything at all. If you're going to get that basic, you might as well go all the way. But then you have to deal with the law. So, you keep the law off your back with latex as thin as a sheet of paper and as close to your body lines as paint.

The band is too loud for any of us to talk, so we just grin at one another like a lot of foreigners. Then Fred's off to get us something from the bar that I don't really want, and he's back in a minute with some screwdrivers, manhattans and martinis. Take your pick. Now booze and I have never gotten along, and that's why I stay away from it. There's nothing moral or ethical about this. I just don't like the taste. Exclamation point, exclamation point, exclamation point. Even a little sip goes straight to my head. So, I plan to nurse this unwanted martini for the rest of the night or just keep it in my hand and not drink it at all.

I just stand there surrounded by all this blasting music and this tangle of bodies and this silly martini in my hand, and somehow I have the feeling that somebody is looking at me. Have you ever had that feeling? It's something you can't explain, but you can actually feel another person's eyes on you. Well, I have this feeling that I'm in somebody's gunsights, and I look to the right and to the left and here and there. No luck east. No luck west. Suddenly I look at the drummer in the band, and it's Tonio. I smile, and he smiles that same half-smile of his and nods. Then he gets really busy with his sticks in the middle of a number that the band is playing. When the piece ends, he looks in my direction again. Our eyes meet for just a second or two. But in that second—I can't explain it—I feel for some crazy reason a little guilty. And I get a queasy feeling in my stomach. It's not the old romantic me any more. It's not the heart-pumping feeling I had with Fred when he called me on the phone. It's as if the old heart-pumping romantic me is dying at that minute, and somebody or something else is taking its place. I try to distract myself, but the feeling doesn't leave me, not for a minute. Anyway, the band starts up again, and Fred asks me to dance. So, I dance for a while with Fred, and then he switches off to dance with Miss Tight-Pants while his buddy dances with me like he's stamping on grapes in a wine-vat. Then I have a few sips of the martini without giving it a thought, and just as I set the martini back on one of the side-tables, the inevitable happens. The floor starts to tip a little to the right and then a little to the left and then it see-saws back and forth like the deck of a ship in a storm. Then I leave Mr. Iron Shoes, and I'm dancing again with Fred. It's a slow piece, and Fred is just as smooth a dancer as he's always been, and I'm floating. I sneak a look at Tonio, and he's watching us. Not spying or looking sideways or anything like that. Just watching. But I can't read the feeling in his eyes one way or the other. Is he angry? Curious? Jealous even? I can't tell. That's Tonio. It's a Mexican trait. They all have that one expression like a passport picture. That's the basic way they face the world, and the expression can change into laughter or hatred in a flash. But when they're in that basic look, you don't know what's on their minds or what's coming next.

Anyway, Fred and I are dancing. I'm feeling tired —maybe because of the martini—, and Fred as usual is just getting warmed up, spinning me around him until I'm dizzy, posing like a matador, doing all these show-biz steps and in general just showing off. He keeps telling me how much he's missed me, how beautiful I look after two years of not seeing me, how good a dancer I still am, how nice it is for him to hold me next to him, the whole litany. It's all just prep talk, and he knows it, and I know it, but I don't know what it's a prep for. At least that what I'm telling myself.

We're packed on that floor like all those crazies on Times Square at midnight on New Year's Eve. It's hard to breathe, let alone dance or even move. Fred and I are waist to waist, and I can feel his hand on my back. He's holding me so hard that it's starting to bother me, and then I feel his hand slide down my hip, and then below my hip. Slow. After a minute he lets the other hand slide down to my waist and then down the other hip, and he has me with both hands down there, and he's pressing me against him so I can feel something happening to him. I don't have to draw you a picture, Carolina. You know men. At the same time I can see that his eyes are getting that glaze on them that men's eyes get when they have just one thing on their minds. For a minute I'm too surprised to push him away from me. Besides I can't push or do much because the other dancers are all pressing against us, front, back and sideways. Just then I notice that the rhythm from the orchestra is different. In fact, there is no rhythm any more—no drum.

The next thing I know—Tonio is beside us, and he has Fred by his yellow shirt and is pushing him away from me. In fact, he pushes him so hard that Fred falls over backward. When Fred gets on his feet, he comes at Tonio with a wild look in his eyes, but Tonio does a little number on him with his hands, and Fred flips down on his back and takes the count. Tonio didn't hit him or anything like that. He just threw him. There must have been some kind of trick to it, but it happened so fast I missed it. I learned later that drummers have arms like firehoses, and the muscles in their arms are like telephone wires. You don't want to tangle with a drummer.

But now the other dancers are watching. I just stand there, and the dizziness is wearing off in a hurry. Tonio is looking at me. I can't tell if he's mad at me or Fred or what the hell, but he sure looks mad. But Tonio always looks mad, like I told you already. He takes a step toward me. Fred is still on the floor where Tonio dropped him, and he's in no hurry to get up, no hurry at all. Tonio is in front of me now. He still looks mad as hell, but he says calmly enough, "I'm sorry I had to butt in like this, but I couldn't watch him handle you like that." Then he turns and marches like a legionnaire through the crowd, and the people separate for him and make a path for him like he was Jesus or Moses or somebody like that.

After a second or two I go out after him, and I catch up to him just before he starts to get into his car. I'm upset, but I don't know if I'm upset because of Fred or because of what happened or what. It really doesn't matter at that point. If you're a woman and you're upset, then you're upset and that's that. Period.

"Why did you raise all that fuss in there and make a scene?" I asked him, but he didn't answer. So, I added, "Who gave you the right to look out for me? I can take care of myself, thank you very much. I've been taking care of myself all my life. I can deal with Fred and a hundred like him, and I don't need any help to do it."

Tonio just looks at me, but I can see that my words aren't having any effect on him at all. "I told you I'm sorry. I'll say it again if it helps. It just bothered me to see him putting his hands on you that way."

"Well, it bothered me too, but I could have dealt with it. I mean with him. What am I supposed to do now? How can I go back in there? That may be your kind of crowd, but it's not mine."

"This isn't my type of gig, Lue. I just came here to do a favor for a friend of mine."

"What difference does that make? You can go back if you want to, but I can't. I can't face those people. And how am I supposed to get home?"

"I'll take you home. If you don't want to go back in or go home with him, I'll take you home."

"Well, you just better, Tonio Vargas. You just better do that."

All the time I'm talking like this I'm wondering why I'm so damn indignant. Frankly, Tonio did me a favor. I wasn't ready for a wrestling match with Fred on that dance floor, and who knows what Fred would have tried later. And then I realized that only somebody who cared about me, really cared about me, would have interfered like that. That's what I thought deep down, but I didn't say it then or ever. What kept coming out of my mouth was how hurt and embarrassed I was and who did Tonio think he was to fight my fights for me.

TONIO brought in two cups of cappuccino while Halleluiah was still facing the reddening darkness where the last inch of the sun was trying not to drown behind the mountains on which it seems to be balancing like an orange globe.

"This cup has a perfect head of foam," he said, holding it for her until he was sure she was gripping the saucered cup by herself. "Do you have it steady, Lue?"

"I can still hold a cup, Tonio," she said, smiling.

He seated himself beside her on the couch again. He deliberately postponed lifting his cup to his mouth until he saw her shakily take her first sip. Some of the foam bubbled and clung to her upper lip. He reached over and wiped the foam away lightly with his forefinger.

"I don't want a wife with a mustache."

"Even a wife with a name like mine."

"What's wrong with your name? Nobody ever forgets it."

"Does it go with Vargas?"

"Hand in glove."

"Imagine. Irish and Mexican. You don't hear about a duo like that every day."

"It's not uncommon, Lue. Do you know the actor, Anthony Quinn?"

"Sure. We had the same last name until I gave it up for you."

"His mother was Mexican, and his father was Irish."

She took another sip of coffee. Again, he wiped the foam from her lip with his fingertip. "Do you know what I was just thinking about?"

"About me, I hope."

"I was thinking of that night when Fred tried to get physical with me out on the dance floor, and you came over and knocked him down. Twice."

"Guilty as charged. Twice," he answered, taking a long sip from his cup that turned into a soft slurp at the end.

"That took a lot of nerve, Tonio."

"Or love."

"Which was it?"

"Both."

"You mean you were sure you loved me then? Absolutely sure?"

"I was sure of that when you spilled iced tea on me on purpose in the cafeteria."

"I never," she said and gave him a mock pout. "Be serious, Tonio. I never did that on purpose, and you know it. Don't keep saying that."

"See. You already have the reaction of the guilty."

"Be serious, sweetheart. When did you really know you loved me?"

"Do you want the truth and nothing but?"

"Nothing but."

"After I drove you home that first night."

"Why? All I did was talk my head off."

"It's not what you said or how much you said or anything like that. It's what I felt. I felt absolutely like myself with you. And I liked the way you put your whole self into everything you said. I don't meet many people like that."

"God, I wish I could say I responded that way. I didn't know how I felt for months."

"That's because you're not a Latino."

"What does that have to do with it?"

"Well, we somehow have it in us that life is basically sad. And at the same time we have the sense that only love can make it happy. That's why we take love seriously when it happens to us. We make time for it. It can last a minute, or it can last a year. The length of time doesn't matter. Either way it stays with you forever."

I KNOW what you're thinking, Carolina. You're probably thinking that the real love story between Tonio and me started when he took me to that flower show or when he put Fred on his backside on the dance floor, right? Well, half right. I mean some of it started there, but that was just ordinary. Maybe I should say it was nothing out of the ordinary. A lot of romances start out that way. Typical but no big deal. But a real love story—and I'm talking from my own experience now—starts where that kind of romance can't go even if it wants to. It just prepares the way, that's all. Of course, big softie that I am, I thought for a long time that romance did all the work, that you just lie back and let it take you and do all the work, but one shock was enough to cure me of that.

It all started about a year and a half ago after I came home from a night class. It was hot, really hot, humid hot. I thought I would just get in the tub and soak into the middle of next week. Müz was visiting her sister down in San Luis Obispo, and Tonio was off with his marching band at some competition in Sacramento, so I had the whole evening with me, myself and I. Muz wouldn't be back until after midnight, and I thought I'd just put on something casual after I got out of the tub and make a light dinner for the two of us and then we'd both go to bed.

The bath was heaven times seven. I remember that just as plain. Woman to woman, Carolina, a bath is like a good kiss. It satisfies you just for what it is. No preparations needed. No promises. You just let yourself go and enjoy it, and for as long as it lasts, you're happy. You know what I mean? I'll bet you've felt that way yourself a lot of times.

I slid down in the tub so that just my milkies and my belly button (mine goes out, not in) and my knees were showing, and I thought how perfectly everything was starting to go for me. I had only half a semester before I finished all my requirements for a degree. Tonio and I were getting to that point where we were really happy only when we were with one another. It didn't matter where we were, just so we were together. That's how far things had progressed for the two of us to that point, and I was starting to learn a lot about what love really means. Do you know what that means? Go ahead, guess. I'll bet you'll never... It means when you're completely happy with someone who is completely happy—complete and happy—with you, and you don't feel you have to talk about it or analyze it or any of that stuff that takes all the fun and the happy sadness out of it. If anybody ever asks you where you heard that, just tell whoever that it's a tip from Halleluiah Quinn Vargas. And it's true to this minute.

Before I go on, have you ever thought how much the telephone means to people who want to be together when they're not. Letters are good, but there's always that delay. With the phone you're in touch—bang, just like that. When I thought I was in love with one of those pre-Tonio guys, I'd like nothing better than to talk on the phone. Sometimes we wouldn't have to say a damn thing. It was enough to know that the other person was on the line, waiting, breathing, thinking about you. That was enough. And I'd hold the receiver and start twisting the receiver cord around my finger or make a bridge out of it when I walked away from the cradle or even twirl it like a skip-rope. You do crazy things when you're on telephone calls that you don't want to end. That never worked with Tonio. He hates telephones. He uses them only when he can't get out of using them. Our real talks are always in person, never on the phone. I hated that at first, not the real talks but that we couldn't continue them on the phone.

I must have stayed in the tub for half an hour. I almost fell asleep there, to tell you the truth. I felt a little woozy, but I blamed that on the humidity. Finally, I decided that I better get out or risk falling asleep right then and there. So up I stood, grabbed a towel and dried myself back, front, face and down the middle creases. Then I really got woozy, and I stopped with the towel until I was myself again. It scared me a little. I should have taken it as a warning, but what did I know?

After I slipped into my robe, I headed for the kitchen. I noticed when I passed the living room clock that it was almost nine o'clock. And that's the last thing I remember.

When I came around, I opened my eyes at floor-level. I was afraid to move. My right hip and right shoulder hurt me. Little by little I tested myself. Right leg? Okay. Left leg? Okay. Right arm? Okay. Left arm? Okay. Neck? Okay. My right side hurt, but I could move, and I guess that I must have landed there when I fell. I still stayed on the carpet and let my eyes do the walking. The living room clock said it was after eleven, so I did a quick calculation. God, two hours plus! Two hours plus, I was on the floor. What did I do—pass out? I'd never passed out in my life before, never even had a dizzy spell. I know girls who pass out when they have their periods, but I never had a problem like that. And I never fainted over anybody or anything. This was a first. Then I felt my left leg start to twitch, and I couldn't stop it. It wasn't violent. It was like that flutter that you get in your eyelid or your cheek sometimes. Everybody gets it. It comes, and then it goes. The twitch in my leg was like that. It was just a vibration, but I couldn't stop it no matter how hard I tried. I even tried to hold it, and it wouldn't stop. Finally, it stopped by itself. Well, that really scared me—scared me in a way I didn't even have a name for.

Is there a word for that in medicine, Carolina? I mean is there a word to describe your body when it does something you don't want it to do? I think there is. But believe you me, when your body gets up and does what it wants and the rest of you is still at the station, you feel more than fear. You feel something like terror. You don't know what it's going to do next. You feel like two different people. First, there's the real you that's still in charge of your life—in charge of what you think is your life. That's the you that plans and remembers things, that has a name and a birthday and a social security number and an address and all the rest of it. And then there's this other you that's in rebellion, that's like a stray sheep that's out of the flock for good, that has a mind and a will of its own.

After five minutes of checking myself out, I started to get up slowly. Really slowly. I turned over on my stomach and scrunched up and back until I was on my knees with my rear end in the air. I kept my head down. I must have been quite a sight with my rear sticking up and my cheek still on the carpet, but I didn't want to take any chances. I was even praying under my breath—all the good old Catholic prayers that Muz taught me when I was growing up. Hail Mary. Our Father. Glory be. All of them. What else is there to do when you're scared by you don't know what? Courage doesn't cut it. Courage is great when you have opposition, when you have something or somebody to fight, but when you don't have anything, you just pray. That's all you have left.

Little by little I raised up the top half of me until I was all the way up and sitting back on my heels. So far so good. So, then I got up the rest of the way until I was on my feet. I was sweating like somebody who's just come out of a steam-room. My robe had come open when I fell, and my whole right side was marked where the carpet weave had stenciled me. Then I remembered that I had started out to make a snack for Muz just before I passed out. And I couldn't think of any reason not to go ahead with that, so that's what I did. Half an hour later Muz came back, and an hour after that we were eating the grilled cheese sandwiches I'd made and drinking coffee, and she was telling me about Aunt Marilyn and Aunt Marilyn's two boys and how beautiful it was in San Luis Obispo. It was always the same story every time Muz came back from a visit with Aunt Marilyn, but I let her tell it again without interrupting her at all because it was the older sister taking about the younger sister, if you know what I mean. But I had another reason that night not to interrupt her. I just wanted to put as much time as possible between what happened to me and the rest of my life.

That one thing taught me a lot about how people react when something goes wrong in their lives. At first you tell yourself that what happened didn't really happen. You just reject it until it almost seems unreal. Then honesty sets in, and you tell yourself that it did happen but that it went away and probably, very probably (you hope), won't come back. Have you ever had a sharp pain in your head or maybe in one of your teeth? It stops you in your tracks, but all of a sudden it goes away. Like that. Instead of seeing it as a warning that something might be wrong, you convince yourself it was just a freak. And you really believe that because you want to believe it. Then you start to get serious about it. You ask a few questions. You read an article. You do a little research in a medical dictionary. You match your symptoms against what you've read. You draw a few conclusions. When you reach that point, you're ready to go to the other extreme. Instead of thinking that a pain in your head or in your tooth is just a passing thing, you convince yourself you have cancer. And then you get hold of yourself and start to work back from that to how you really feel. That's the way it goes. From nothing to the worst thing possible. Then the needle steadies on the truth. Either way you're at the mercy of the facts, and eventually you come face to face with them and do what you have to do. There's no escape, really.

I never told Muz about what happened that night. Maybe I should have, but I didn't. But a week later I mentioned to Tonio that a friend of mine had passed out for a couple of hours and then had gotten up and just gone about her business and what did he think of that? Tonio always listens closely, Carolina, when you talk to him about problems. He's tuned in to problems because that's what he deals with every day where he works. One problem after another. That's what teachers have to do these days. They're sensitive to problems, and they know that some problems have answers and some problems don't. Tonio just listened to me and didn't say anything for a long time, but his expression changed. Not changed. Deepened. You know what I mean? Then he looked up at me and asked, "So you passed out for couple of hours?"

"Not me, Tonio. A friend of mine."

"Don't play games with me, Lue."

"I'm not."

"Don't do that. I don't want that kind of thing between us. Just talk to me."

"Well," I said finally. My voice wasn't my own just then. You know how you get when you're trapped in your own lie. "All right, I fainted. I was the one. Everybody faints once in a while. I was just wondering about it, that's all."

"Did you see a doctor?"

"No."

"How long were you out? Unconscious, I mean? Did you fall? Did you hurt yourself? Were you alone?"

"One at a time, Tonio."

"Did you hurt yourself?"

"No."

"How long were you out?"

"Not long."

"How long? Five minutes? When you were telling me about your friend, you said she was out for a couple of hours. Was it that long? How long were you out?"

"How would I know? I didn't time myself."

"Why did you say a couple of hours before?"

"It was longer than five minutes, but I..."

"Damn it, Lue, stop evading me."

It was the first time I saw anger in Tonio's eyes—anger aimed at me. It really frightened me. "More than an hour."

The anger faded immediately. He looked right into my eyes, and his look was like a doctor's look. Then he turned away. I could actually feel him thinking.

"It hasn't happened again, has it?"

"No."

"Is that the truth?"

"Cross my heart."

He stood up and started to pace, and his thinking seemed to fill the whole room. "I think it might be a good idea, Lue, if you make an appointment with a doctor. I know one. She's Mexican like me. We grew up together. Her name is Carolina Pacheco. I'll call her."

CAROLINA PACHECO did not look or sound Mexican at all. It was only when she spoke that there was a hint of a vowel here or there that was longer or broader than usual. Her hair was light brown, and she had a complexion that looked as if the sun would burn rather than tan it. Her teeth, like Tonio's, were unbelievably white, perfectly aligned and flawless.

"I'm sorry I had to put you through such an examination," she said, "but that really tells me more sometimes than anything I might get from the lab."

"I've never been examined like that in my life," said Halleluiah, tucking her blouse back into her skirt and seating herself opposite Carolina, who was making notations on a clipboard.

"How long have you and Tonio been..." Carolina began.

"Just eight months."

"Did he tell you we were raised together? By the way, how do you want me to call you?"

"Lue. Everybody but my father says Lue."

"If I call you Lue, would you call me Carolina? Actually, Carolina Maria Isabel Pilar Pacheco, if you want the whole litany." She paused and smiled, and her smile made Halleluiah smile back. "Anyway, did Tonio tell you we were raised together?"

"He did."

"We were next door neighbors actually. That was back in Nuevo Laredo before the family migrated to California. We were dirt poor then. You can't imagine." She paused again and made several more notations on the board.

"Tonio never told me much about his family. He takes care of his father. I know that. I've met his father. As a matter of fact, I'm meeting Tonio and his father again tonight."

"Well, that's Tonio's whole family now. Just his father. His mother died when we crossed over into Texas the year before we all came to Los Angeles. There was a younger sister named Lourdes, but she died as an infant." She looked up. "Tonio's father worked as a migrant laborer when we first came here. And Tonio worked too from the time he was that high." She held her hand out, table-high. "In fact, I can't remember a time when Tonio wasn't working. Setting pins in a bowling alley, selling newspapers, doing all kinds of laboring jobs when he was still a teenager. Even now he plays drums two or three nights a week while he's teaching and finishing his graduate work. His father's of an age now when he just wants to work in his garden and spend the evenings with other Mexican men his age. They smoke out on the porch and talk about the old days."

"I've only seen Tonio play drums once, and that was at a country club dance that ended up in a fight."

"He's a wonderful drummer. I've never seen Tonio fight, but I wouldn't want to be the one who crossed him." Carolina placed the clipboard on top of her desk and stood up. Halleluiah watched her expression change from friendly to dispassionate and professional.

"What I'm really interested in right now, Carolina, is what you're going to tell me about me."

Carolina smiled reassuringly, "Actually there's not much I can tell you at this point. I don't detect anything unusual from this exam. You've told me that you don't remember anything about the time you fainted except that you did. You don't remember anything like a seizure. You just passed out. The length of time you were out concerns me, but that might have other explanations. Fatigue. menstruation..."

"I wasn't having my period then if that's what you're driving at."

"Well, that eliminates that." She came closer to Halleluiah and stood squarely in front of her. She put her hands softly on her shoulders. "Have you felt any numbness anywhere since the day you passed out?"

"No." She paused. "Well, there was a little soreness in my right arm when I came to on the carpet, but I just assumed that that was because I was lying on it. It went away."

"I don't mean soreness. I mean numbness, lack of feeling."

"No, nothing like that."

"Don't make light of it if you have the slightest suspicion, Lue. Talk to me like your sister. That's the way I want us to be. Like sisters."

"I'm not hiding anything, Carolina."

"Does your mother know you're seeing me?"

"No."

"Don't you think she should know?"

"Why? It might be nothing. You don't know Muz. She'd be scared to death."

"Well, she is your mother..." She paused. "This could be serious, Lue."

"I thought you didn't find anything wrong."

"I said 'could be.' Any time a person passes out for a couple of hours, there has to be some concern about..."

"About what?"

"About what a routine examination can't discover. We have to go step by step."

"What's the next step?"

"A CAT scan."

"When?"

"As soon as I can arrange an appointment. Tomorrow maybe."

"You really mean that?"

"Yes, Lue, I do."

WHAT I didn't tell you during that first examination, Carolina, was that Tonio and I were pretty tight with one another by then. After those first few dates, we had been seeing one another a lot—first, once a week, then twice a week, then almost every day. And if we didn't see one another, we'd call. I mean I'd call. I've already told you about Tonio and telephones.

I introduced him to Muz. She was a little surprised. I have to be frank with you. It was because he was Mexican. Muz always told me that she didn't have a prejudice against anyone, but it's a different story when it comes close to home. For a long time her prejudices got the better of her. She said once that if I married him and had a daughter, the girl might have really hairy legs and even a mustache. It sounds so wrong and silly when I write it out like this, but mothers can think of some far-out things to say to a girl sometimes when things aren't going the way they thought they would go. They think they have your best interest at heart, and in their minds they do, I suppose. They think that what they're saying is going to make you think more, make you cautious. It ends up being plain annoying.

It wasn't long before all that stuff went out the window. When Muz really got to know Tonio, she thought more of him than I did. He had all those qualities that men like my Dad didn't even know existed. He was as patient as the stars, and he always seemed to anticipate whatever you might need just when you needed it, and if he said he'd be some place, that's sure as hell where he would be. You could set your wristwatch by him. Dependable. That's Tonio. Dependable.

About a month before I came for that examination in your office, Tonio and I talked about marriage. Tonio did the talking or rather the asking. I just listened. But let me start at the beginning, not the end. One night, Tonio and I were going to see the Dodgers out at the ravine. He came early because he wanted me to meet his father. While we were driving over to his house, Tonio started to tell me what he really felt about me. I can't remember his words, but they did a job on me. I did what I do a lot of. I started to cry. I mean I started to cry and couldn't stop myself.

"Did I say it wrong?" Tonio asked me.

"No, you said it too right. In fact, it was so right I couldn't help myself. I need a handkerchief. Please."'

"I have something better than a handkerchief."

Tonio leaned over after he said that and kissed me on each eye, tears and all, and at that minute, Carolina, I'd have cut off my right arm for him. It got to me, and he always gets to me that way. Right through the heart. It's not a strategy or a ploy or anything like that. It's the way he thinks. No, it's the way he says and does what he feels. Exactly. Maybe it's a carryover from music. I don't know. I don't even want to know. But he's something, I tell you. It's almost unfair because when he does that you don't have any defense. I know what you're thinking. You're ready to ask me why does a girl need a defense? Well, I don't know why. Maybe it's just because we like to think we do.

This all happened while we were on the way to visit his father. For the first time, remember. I was scared wobbly. I asked Tonio to give me a few hints, a few pointers, but he ignored me. I must have jabbered all the way to his house. I was that nervous. When I'm nervous, I talk. Are you like that? Probably not. But a lot of women are, and I'm sure as hell one of them.

We pull up in front of the house, and there's Tonio's father on the porch. He's wearing a white shirt and a plain blue tie. I can see that he's just shaved and combed his hair. But he's sitting, and he has a cane across his lap. Tonio opens the car door for me, and we start up to the porch. I look up and see that his father is watching me. He's not staring at me or looking me over, nothing like that. I don't feel any question marks in his look. No, he's just letting his eyes take me in the way you might welcome somebody into your living room. He was taking me into himself, and I just walked right into his eyes, if you know what I mean. When we're a few steps in front of him, Tonio goes ahead and kisses his father on the lips, and I can hear the two of them talking in Spanish. Then Tonio turns back to me and smiles, and his father takes hold of his cane, plants it so he can lean on it and stands up for me, slowly.

Tonio's father has skin that has—don't think I'm crazy when I write this—a blue tint to it. He's very dark. I don't know if it's from the sun or just natural, or maybe he's spent so much of his life in the sun that it's all turned into the same thing. He has that kind of black hair that used to be called Indian hair. It wants to stay black forever. Tonio's father hardly has a gray hair in his head. He has a face like Tonio's, the skin tight over his face-bones like drumskin on a drumhead, no slack anywhere. And he never seems to blink. His eyes find you, and they rest on you. They don't weigh on you. It's not that kind of look. You almost feel, I don't know, honored.

Tonio's already briefed his father, I know. So, when I put out my hand, Mr. Vargas shifts his cane from his right to his left hand and takes my hand in his right hand. His grip is so soft, but it's sure at the same time. I feel as if my hand is inside a rabbit-fur-lined glove, that soft.

"Encantado, señorita."

"Igualmente," I say, and I just hope that my Spanish doesn't sound too American.

"Ah ha, habla español, señorita?"

"Sí."

"Bueno."

After that it's all downhill. Mr. Vargas is not much of a talker, but he's the best listener in the whole world. He doesn't just listen with his ears. He listens with his eyes. Do you understand? But you've known him all your life. You must know what I'm talking about.

I really want him to like me, but it's hard for me to tell. People think that Mexicans are very quick to be happy and laugh and all that, but that's not the way it is. They're really very laid back, especially in the beginning, very conservative, very concerned about not being too familiar too quickly. At least that's what I've found.

Tonio's already prepped me that his father's English is not enough to write home about, so I'm using every bit of Spanish I know to keep things moving along. Finally, just when I'm about to run out of gas, Mr. Vargas puts his hand on my hand and says, "Señorita, no es necesario hablar todo el tiempo. Me gusta estar con usted y Tonio. Es bastante."

Here he's telling me that I don't have to talk all the time and that all he wants is just to be with Tonio and me, and what have I been doing but talking his ear off? So I just pipe down, and everything is just fine. Finally, when it's time to leave, Mr. Vargas walks with Tonio and me to the car. Tonio tells him we're gong to the Dodger game, then he kisses him goodnight the same way he kissed him hello, and then, I don't know, I kiss him, too. Even while I'm doing it, I feel I'm being too forward and that I'm probably bollixing the whole thing, but Mr. Vargas drops his cane and holds me by the shoulders while I'm kissing him, and he does it so softly, so gently. It's his way of embracing me, I think, so I return it. Then I pull back. Mr. Vargas has tears in his eyes, but he's smiling at the same time. And just at that minute I know that he likes me.

Well, that's the story about the first visit with Mr. Vargas, Carolina. But would you believe it that ever since that first time, he always holds me the same way when I'm ready to leave. By the shoulders, and he lets me kiss him, and afterward he is smiling, and he has tears in his eyes.

So off we drove to the ravine for the game. The Dodgers lost to the Cardinals in fourteen innings. The worst kind of way to end an evening, with that kind of loss. And they had a million chances to win it, but they blew it. Typical. I take baseball seriously, and I was feeling definitely down because our reliever balked in a run in the fourteenth inning. Tonio though was quiet. In fact, he'd been quiet during the whole game. I figured he was looking at the fine points because he really understands and appreciates the game, while I'm just your basic fan. In fact, Tonio's in a league. What position do you think he plays? Go ahead, guess. You'll never. Well, I'll just tell you. Catcher. Doesn't that fit Tonio?

While we were heading back to the car, Tonio stopped and looked up at the sky. The night was totally clear, and it looked like every star in the universe was trying to get into the act up there. Tonio was taking it all in, and I stopped to take it all in too. There was one star moving in from the sea, but that turned out to be a jet circling for a landing at LAX.

When Tonio turned to me, he had that inspired look he gets right after he's listened to good music.

"You know, Lue, when the sky is this big and the stars are that clear and that many, it makes me feel as if we're the only two people in the world."

"What if," I said, just to be clever, "what if we were the only two people in the world?"

"Then maybe I wouldn't have to ask you what I'm going to ask you. Maybe it just would be taken for granted."

"That's too deep for me, Tonio."

He smiled, and his teeth were twice as white in the darkness than they were under the lights in the stadium. "Lue," he said, "how would you feel about being married to a band director?"

A proposal in a parking lot. Where was the candlelight dinner and the music in the background and the flowers on the table, and all the rest of it? But a parking lot? I couldn't make the connection for a minute. Then I realized that the stars and the sky were the real setting for Tonio. The parking lot didn't even register.

"How would you feel?" he asked again.

Well, you can just about guess what I did. I felt the tears coming, and I just sat down on the front bumper of a Toyota and cried like I do at the opera. Only this time it was the real thing. Some people who were passing just stopped dead and looked at me to see if anything was wrong. I think they thought Tonio bopped me or something. But I smiled at them through the tears to show them I was all right, and they kept on walking. Tonio stayed beside me the whole time and kept his hand on my shoulder until I cried myself dry.

"Tonio," I said when I was back to normal again. "please don't ever do that to me again when we're in public like this. I can't help myself."

"But you didn't answer."

"Promise me you won't do it again."

"That depends on your answer."

"What depends on my answer?"

"Whether I'll ever do it again. I'll just keep proposing to you after a ball game out in the open like this until you say yes."

"Okay, then, yes."

"Is that your answer?"

"Yes."

"Just like that?"

"Yes."

"Do you always answer serious questions with just one word like that?"

"Yes."

"Is that your last word?"

"Yes."

"Can I count on that?"

"Yes."

"If I asked you in Spanish, would you give me the same answer?"

"Yes."

"Quieres casarme, Lue? Do you want to marry me?"

"Sí."

"Sí?"

"Sí, sí, sí."

CAROLINE aligned several sheets of paper beside a thin stack of x-rays on her desk. After she aligned them, she touched them askew and re-aligned them. Tonio watched her do this from his seat on the opposite side of the desk.

"Tonio," Carolina said, facing him. "I've checked and re-checked the x-rays and the reports. I know the technicians who did these. They don't make mistakes, and there's no mistake this time."

Tonio's expression did not change. He had been staring steadily past Carolina's face as she spoke, concentrating on a whiff of cloud that was coasting past the window.

"I wish you had never asked me to see her, Tonio," Carolina said.

"Why? You were the one doctor I knew I could trust more than any other."

"I knew that's the way you felt, but I shouldn't have said yes. I wish she'd gone to someone else. She's sweet. She's so open. Now I have to tell her what I've found. I've gotten to be as close to her as a sister. This won't be easy for me."

"Do you have to tell her?"

"What do you mean?"

"Do you have to tell her everything?"

"What choice is there? There has to be surgery. She has to know why. And after the surgery there will be chemotherapy and radiation. There's no way I can keep the truth from her."

"Why don't you tell her there has to be surgery and leave it go at that?"

"For now that's all I intend to say. There's no sense telling her everything that might be in store for her."

"This is terrible, Carolina. This is the worst thing. I know the effect this will have on her."

"Tonio, I'll be as considerate as I can, I promise. but you can't hide things from intelligent people, especially from intelligent people who are friends. That's why I told you I wish you had never sent her to me. I'm her friend, but I'm also her doctor. I have responsibilities. It's a matter of ethics for me. I know the kind of tumor I'm dealing with here."

"Does she have to know?"

"I don't see how I can keep it from her."

"Just say it's a tumor. Don't say what kind it is. Do this for me. You won't be lying."

"But what if that doesn't satisfy her?"

"Then do what you have to do."

Tonio stood and walked to the door. He opened it and turned back to Carolina. "I'm still going to go ahead with the wedding."

"Is that wise after what I've told you?"

"Wise?"

"She has a tumor, Tonio."

"But she's still the same person, isn't she?"

"What if she doesn't want the wedding? Have you talked to her?'

"That's where I'm going now."

"Don't you think it's better if I talk to her first? I've scheduled the operation for Saturday."

"Saturday? That soon?"

"That's standard procedure, Tonio. Time is our enemy in this case."

"All right, you talk to her first. I'll talk to Paco and ask him if he can marry us on Friday. All the paperwork and tests are finished. I'll explain the facts to him. He'll understand."

"I still feel you should think more about this. Both of you. What do you lose if you wait?"

"Time."

I'D HEARD that people who are shot sometimes don't realize they've been shot even after they see blood. That's how I felt after you told me there was something wrong in my head. I walked into your office as healthy as you please, and I left like somebody who'd been sentenced or something. Try to imagine. No, don't. You'll never. It has to happen to you.

Even now it all seems like a dream to me. Maybe I should say nightmare. And it's still going on. We both know that.

I think the only thing that got me through that day was knowing how hard it was for you to tell me. I almost felt I had to keep your spirits up, and I'm not the best spirit-keeper-upper in this world, I kid you not.

When I walked home, I felt the world wasn't my friend any more. Can you believe that? It was the same world I'd lived in all my life, but in just a few minutes it made me see myself as an outsider, somebody it was ready to dispense with. I felt like someone who has been accused of the worst kind of thing but who's innocent. I felt innocent but that no one would believe me. That kind of feeling. And I was wondering how I would tell Muz. Or Tonio.

I wanted to be with somebody, but I still wanted to be by myself. I felt that if I didn't tell anybody and kept it my secret, it would go away, that I'd wake up and it would be gone. Just like a nightmare. In fact, when I did get up the next morning, that was the worst feeling of all, to know it was still there, to know that every day I lived before that day was something like a gift, or a loan, or just a warm-up for the real thing.

The first thing I thought of was dying, Carolina. Before it was just an idea. Now it had a name and a timetable. I thought my life was over. I mean I thought I was already dead but that I had a little time to accept the idea.

You want to know the truth? I still haven't accepted it.

"SIT DOWN, Tonio," said the priest. "We can talk here."

They were in the priest's dining room. The nuns already had the table set for dinner. There was a vase of lilacs in the middle of the table. The priest sat in a chair on one side of the table and gestured for Tonio to sit at the head.

"You're a groom-to-be, Tonio. You'll be the head of your house. You should get used to sitting at the head of the table."

Tonio reversed the chair with one hand, straddled it easily and faced the priest like a penitent in a confessional.

"You think I'm loco, verdad?" Tonio asked, his chin resting on his crossed arms on top of the chair back.

"No."

"Tell me the truth, Paco. I'm not looking for moral support or anything like that, but I'd like to know. Friend to friend."

"What I think doesn't matter. What you think matters."

"Then why did you ask me in here? We've taken care of all the details for Friday."

The priest stood and walked slowly around the table until he was standing behind Tonio, who did not turn around to face him.

"We're the same age, amigo. We come from the same home town. We've grown up together." He paused. "Do you remember when I told you in Laredo that I was going to the seminary, the novitiate?"

Tonio turned. He looked surprised.

"Do you remember?" the priest repeated.

"Yes, I remember."

"You and I must have talked for more than an hour down by the river. Remember? It was summer, and the Rio Grande was so low you could wade across it. I told you I was going to be a priest. You didn't discourage me. You just asked me questions to make sure I was sure about what I wanted to do, about my vocation."

"I'd forgotten all about that, Paco."

"And they were the best questions. They made me think hard about what I was going to do, and I was stronger for it afterward. I didn't realize it at the time, but I do now."

The priest came back to his chair, turned it around and straddled it as Tonio had done. For a moment the two men sat looking at one another like two schoolboys in a deserted cafeteria.

"You'll be entering a difficult time in your life, Tonio. Even when two people are perfectly healthy, marriage can be difficult."

The priest waited to see how Tonio would respond, but Tonio just looked at the floor between the two of them.

"Are you strong enough?" continued the priest. "Strong in your heart, I mean, to face what you might have to face?"

"I don't know, Paco." Tonio raised his eyes. "All I know if that I can't think any other way. I can't imagine any other life for myself. How can I say this? When I'm not with her, I'm only half of my-self."

"But do you have to marry her because of that? Especially now with what you are facing, what you both are facing?"

"In my heart I'm already married to her, and I have been since I first met her. All I want you to do is pronounce us."

"Does she want this, too?"

"In her heart she does, but she thinks now I'm going though with this because I feel sympathy for her."

"Do you?"

"All this just makes me love her more, Paco. It makes me want to help and fight more. I have to face this with her. Anything else, and I couldn't live with myself. I can't say it any other way than that."

The priest looked directly at Tonio until their eyes met. "And the worst? What if the worst happens?"

Tonio looked down at the floor. For several minutes he said nothing. Then, still looking at the floor, he said, "I used to think like everybody, Paco. I thought you married, and your whole life was ahead of you. Now I don't think that you marry for your whole life, but with your whole life. Time doesn't have anything to do with it. There is no time to come except in our head. There's only right now. Right now could go on for fifty minutes or fifty years. Nobody can control that. All you can control is how you feel and act for every minute or every day you're given. That's how I look at Lue and me. That's how I looked at it before I knew she was sick. This only makes it more definite."

"Is that the truth?"

Tonio kissed his thumb. "It's how I feel, how I've felt from the beginning..."

"Well, then," said the priest, standing and situating the chair at its proper position at the table. "I think we've said all that can be said." He waited until Tonio stood, put his arm around his shoulders and walked slowly with him to the door. "Sometimes we don't know how God tries us, Tonio. None of us knows. But I have a feeling that you've been given a special calling, a special grace. Maybe God chose you for this girl for a special reason, and it could be that her sickness is the reason. That takes a different kind of love, and you are the only one I've ever known who has it." He removed his hand and walked silently for several steps. "I'll be remembering you both at Mass every day from now on. I want you to know that."

"Thank you, Paco."

I KEPT feeling the shaved spot on the top of my head where the needle went in. Things were happening so fast that my mind was playing catch-up to what was happening to my body and not doing a very good job of it. First, there was that meeting in your office when you examined me. Then there was the biopsy. Then I had to explain things to Muz, and she just about died. That was the worst time for me.

Tonio was like the Rock of Gibraltar. He didn't even flinch when I told him, just held me close to him as if I would balloon off somewhere if he let go of me. I still think that you gave him the news before I did, Carolina. He looked prepared. But that doesn't matter. He just kept telling me this was a routine procedure, just precautionary, that a biopsy was just a follow-up, stuff like that. He wouldn't let me dwell on it and he didn't leave me by myself for a minute.

I kept thinking how tough it must have been for you, Carolina, to level with me. Believe me, it would have been just as hard for me if I was in your shoes.

You were a real pro, and I loved you for it, and I still love you for it. But what threw me for a loop was the wedding. Tonio still wanted to go though with it. We'd just move everything up. He'd talked to Father Sanchez, and everything was okay on that end. Well, you can guess the first thing I thought. Knowing Tonio, I figured he was doing this because he had promised me or felt sorry for me or something like that. I mean I felt he thought he was obligated. In fact, I told him that face to face when we talked about it that Wednesday before the wedding.

"Tonio," I said. "I know you love me, but I can't let you prove it this way. It's too much—over and above. Let's see how things work out. What's to be gained your way? We get married on Friday, and the next morning I'm on the operating table. What's the sense in that?"

"There's no sense in it. There'd be more sense in waiting, but that means we're not in control any more. Why should we let something like this dictate how we live? Why? If we put it in the driver's seat now, that's where it's going to stay."

That was Tonio's argument, and he never changed it. He's still the same this minute. But here I was facing surgery, and here was Tonio saying we should get married regardless. He'd made all the arrangements with Father Sanchez for the wedding. I mean the service. We knew there wouldn't be anything but a service. Just Muz and Tonio's father and you and that was it. After we found out that you couldn't be there, there was just the four of us. So, we went to Father Sanchez' church and were married just like that in English and Spanish. After, we went to a restaurant in Claremont for dinner. Then Tonio drove Muz and his father home and drove me straight to the hospital. That was my wedding night, checking into the hospital and getting my head shaved and feeling that plastic I.D. wristband catching the little hairs on my wrist. Tonio stayed with me the whole time. He wouldn't even leave me the next morning when they were getting me ready. The last thing I remember was the way he held my hand in his hand—just the way his father held my hand, so soft but so sure—when they wheeled me on that cold gurney into the operating room. Everything was so bright in there—the walls, the shining metal things, and all that equipment. You came over and kissed me, Carolina, remember? That was my anchor.

Now I look back on the operation as the easy part. The hard part was the chemo and the radiation that came later. They made me so sick. I just couldn't get the better of it. First there'd be the nausea. Then I'd throw up, and then everything would come out the other ends of me like there was nothing to stop it. I lived in the bathroom. I'd lean my forehead on the sink-top because the porcelain was so cool. It made me want to die. Really want to die, pray to die. I just reached a point where I started to wonder if it was all worth it. The stakes kept getting higher and higher, and each day was more and more difficult, and nothing was getting any simpler. I just wanted to float away and come back to things as they were. To be re-born, you know? Of course, that was just a dream, but it kept me from feeling completely locked in. And, believe me, I was locked in. You can't plan. You don't even want to plan. You just want to have a few minutes when you don't feel seasick, when you stop heaving for a little while, when you don't have to sit on the toilet because you're afraid to get up. You just go from hour to hour, daylight to darkness. Short stints.

I got so sick of that hospital room. The same ceiling. The same walls. The same every damn thing. No wonder people hate hospitals. Muz just cried every time she came to see me so I told her to visit Aunt Marilyn in San Luis Obispo. At least for the time being. And she did, finally, but it wasn't easy to convince her.

But Tonio stayed with me day and night. Whenever he wasn't working, he was with me. He only left to sleep, and sometimes not even then. He could get pretty stubborn about it, especially when I was having a bad time. He'd stay and sleep off and on all night in the chair beside my bed. They would quote the regulations to him, and then they would insist, but they didn't know Tonio. He would stay on his own terms, and he would leave on his own terms, and that was when he was good and ready, regulations or no regulations. Nobody was ever going to tell him what to do where I was concerned. That's what I love about him, Carolina. He lives by his own rules, and eventually the other rules bend to his. I don't know how he does it, but he does it. Persistence, I guess.

Have you ever noticed how rules can always be changed, but it has to come from the top down. Most rules, anyway. It's like they exist to keep everybody in line except the ones who have the power to change them. Tonio told me that. That's why he decides when and where to take on the power himself. He does it on sheer will. And he stays with it until things come his way. He told me once that there is a limited number of no's that an individual is capable of saying. So, you keep after your opponent until he runs out of no's and then you'll get the answer you want. I've seen him in action that way, and his theory works. He doesn't do it unless he thinks he's absolutely right about something, but once he thinks he's right, he doesn't budge an inch.

I had a lot of time to think in the hospital, and the main thing I thought about wasn't living or dying. I read somewhere that cancer is just one death after another, and I wasn't ready to go down that road, so I took my mind off it. I knew I was in good hands, and I felt that with luck I could come through. The odds were fifty-fifty. Not good, but not hopeless either.

Of course, I didn't want to look at myself in the mirror after they took the bandages off my head. It took me days before I had the nerve. And when I did, I broke down and cried like a widow. You were there. Remember? You kept telling me that it would grow back, it would grow back. But I wouldn't let Tonio see me that way. Like some plucked chicken with a zipper scar on the top of my head. I asked for some hand towels, and made a kind of babushka or turban out of them and covered myself like that whenever Tonio was with me. It's the old female strategy, Carolina. Vanity first, vanity last. If you don't like the way you look, you can still play a few tricks on the world. To tell you the truth, it pleased me to know that I had some vanity left. But even with the hand towels I was no bargain. I looked like a little nun. Looks mean something to a woman, and I couldn't stand myself. Maybe it's the same for men. I don't know about that. But I always believed that looking like you want to look changes your whole personality, your whole view of yourself. You feel like yourself, and that keeps you from feeling like what you've been made to look like, what you've become. It's not as important as courage, that's for damn sure, but it's right up there. Courage is still the king of the hill. If you lose that, you've lost everything, right? There are times when I feel like I'm losing what little courage I have, and I just pray that I don't come apart. I cry alone and when I'm done, I feel as if nothing's left, nothing at all. But just when I think everything's gone and I'm down to ground zero, some little courage-bud starts to sprout. It's as if I have to reach that point to make it happen, as if it doesn't happen until you need it. That's a funny thing about human nature, isn't it? Something is created by nothing, and you don't even know how it exists until it exists. I remember once I was watching Muz knit a sweater. She did the same thing with her fingers and the needles, over and over and over. I told her that I wouldn't have the patience to do that. And she said that doing it gives you the patience. You don't have it in advance. It's the same with courage. But it's a mixed blessing. Sometimes I even hate to have the courage I have left because all it does is make me strong enough to face something that broke my life in two. What good is courage if it just makes you strong enough to see the worst possible thing that could happen? But then again what's the alternative? A bottle of sleeping pills?

My love story isn't like any of the big ones, Carolina. It's not full of heavy breathing and jewelry and all that, but it's a lot better, and it's all mine. I'm telling you this because only someone who's like a sister would understand it. It's a wonderful thing to know you're loved by someone you love. I almost feel that I don't deserve it—like it's a gift I don't really have coming to me. But I'd be zero without it. Absolute zero, sub-zero. It's all I live for.

To see Tonio come through that door and just look at me—the me that's really inside of my skin and not the one that everybody else sees. That's what completes me. And that's happiness. Even if I died in the next hour, I'd die knowing that I knew what happiness was in my life, what love is. There's nothing else. And if it only happens to you for a single minute, that single minute is a life-time, a complete life-time. That might sound like something out of an old movie, Carolina, but it's true. It happens to me every day.

MORNINGS were the worst time for her. Tonio usually would not arrive at the hospital before two in the afternoon, and Halleluiah had to busy herself with something or other to pass the time until he came. On scheduled days there would be the sickening therapy. On other days there would be nothing for her to do. She tried to read on a regular basis, but reading made her think, and thinking bought her face to face with her condition. After a week she had no motivation to read anything but the newspapers, and the daytime television programs bored her completely.

At the beginning of the third week, she awoke as usual. This was not a therapy day, so she was immediately relieved. When her breakfast tray was brought in, she ate all the cereal and toast. By the time she reached for the coffee, it was cold. In a way she was relieved because this gave her a reason not to drink it. She missed Tonio's cappuccino more than she could say.

She never knew exactly when she went to sleep, but when she opened her eyes, she saw Tonio's father seated in one of the two chairs for visitors at the foot of the bed. His eyes were closed, and she studied the lines and creases and slants of his face as if it were the face of an Egyptian potentate. It had the same undisguisable simplicity and resignation and dignity. She wondered if she should say something. Then she decided against it, but she continued to watch. She could see that his lips were moving slightly, and she knew at once that he was praying. Suddenly she realized that he had come by himself to the hospital just so he could pray for her. But how had he come? Who had brought him? She watched his eyelids flutter briefly, and she thought he was going to look at her, but instead the eyelids remained closed.

More than fifteen minutes passed, and the old man remained in the chair, his eyelids pressed shut, his lips shaping the words he was speaking in silence.

Halleluiah remembered the two visits she had made to Tonio's house and how his father on both occasions had maintained a kind of reserve. He did not stare at her then, but his eyes never left her. Then she remembered how he placed his hands on her shoulders when she said goodnight to him and how she knew instinctively at that moment that he not only accepted her but approved of her, loved her without any further questions, wanted her for his son.

Now as she watched him in his chair, she had the same feeling of acceptance and reassurance. She felt at the same time that he had come to fulfill a promise to himself and that it would be better if she did not interrupt him as he did so. She closed her eyes, pretending that she was asleep.

After several minutes, she heard him stand, heard the firm tap of the cane on the hospital floor, then heard his slow shuffling steps as he came closer to the head of the bed. She fought to keep her eyes closed. Then she felt his hand on her forehead, and it had the same lightness and warmth that she remembered. It remained on her forehead for just an instant. Then, as he lifted it, he made a small sign of the cross just above her eyebrows.

Halleluiah waited. She could sense that he was looking down at her. Then she heard him shuffle away. When she opened her eyes slowly, carefully, almost fearfully, she saw that he was again seated in the same chair. He was leaning forward slightly, his hands on his lap, his eyes closed. He looked so tired that she thought he might be about to fall forward. It made her want to throw back the sheet and blanket that covered her and rush to him and support him. But she stayed where she was, keeping her eyelids half closed so that she could close them all the way if he should suddenly look up at her. But he never did. A minute or two more went by, and then he stood, blessed himself in the Mexican way by kissing his thumb-top at the end of the sign of the cross and left the room. Tap, shuffle, tap, shuffle, tap, tap, tap.

Later in the afternoon when Tonio arrived, Hallelujah said, "Your father was here this morning."

"Here? How did he get here?'

"I don't know, but he was here, and he sat right there for more than half an hour and then he left."

"Did you talk?"

"I pretended I was asleep."

"You mean you didn't talk to one another?" he asked as he vased a bouquet of white carnations that he had brought with him. He centered the vase on the windowsill. "I wonder if he took a cab or got Diego to drive him over."

"I know why he came, Tonio."

"Why?"

"He came to pray for me."

After a pause Tonio said, "I wouldn't be surprised. He does that. He believes in that."

"Don't you?"

"Not the way he does."

IT FELT like forever before I was allowed to leave that hospital, before good old bald me was wheeled to the front door and then helped into Tonio's car even though I didn't need a bit of help by that time. But those are the rules. Get them out of the hospital in one piece, and then they're on their own, right? I graduated from patient to out-patient. You were optimistic, Carolina, and that was enough for me. You told me I was clean as far as all the possible tests could determine, but that I'd have to come regularly just to keep a close tab on developments.

I was so damn anxious to get home—Tonio's home and mine too now. I kept having to tell myself that I was married, that I had a new address. Tonio had rented a place not too far from where he lived with his father, and he'd been fixing it up and furnishing it so that it would be ready when I was released, and I must say, Carolina, that he outdid himself. Talk about being complete! When I came in the front door and saw how clean and beautiful everything was, I almost lost it. Not almost. I lost it.

I sat there and bawled like a nursery, and Tonio just stood beside me for a minute or two until I got over it. Why in the hell do I cry all the time when I'm happy? Answer me that, will you? Of course, sad things make me cry, but that's true for everybody. But happy things? Every time one of them happens to me, I just blubber.

The whole house was on one floor—no split level, no sunken rooms, nothing but dead even. That was Tonio's way of telling me that I wouldn't have to worry about steps. Remember? You told him that I might have some trouble with depth perception. Well, that stuck, and he thought a house without any steps would take care of that problem pronto. The living room had a sofa and two chairs, and the kitchen was painted the color of buttermilk, and the bedroom was like something you'd tie a ribbon around and give to some good friend for Christmas. Wall to wall white carpet and white walls the same color and a bed with a bedspread the color of butterscotch and a dressing table with all my war paint and other things already lined up there. I figured that Muz must have helped Tonio with that, but I didn't ask. Some things you don't ask about. You just appreciate. Asking questions would spoil everything.

After Tonio gave me a tour of the house, he brought me back to the living room and got me nice and settled on the sofa and just left me to my thoughts. I knew what he was going to do. He was going to make some cappuccino. I was right. In just a minute or two I could smell the coffee from the kitchen. He must have had it ready and waiting.

I kept the babushka on my head. I'd really gotten used to it, and it gave me a kind of security, even with Tonio. I should say especially with Tonio. Without it I felt almost ashamed. Well, ashamed might be too strong a word. Let's just say I felt embarrassed. Embarrassed the way you might feel if you were caught naked some place and couldn't cover yourself. You know. Embarrassed.

So Tonio and I sat in our new living room and drank cappuccino, and it was just like it was supposed to be. Just the way I had hoped it would be. In fact, I had spent so much time imagining what we were doing right then, I felt when we did it, I felt that it was a re-run. Deja vu. It's hard to explain to anyone who hasn't been through it, but all the agony of the post-op, and then all the therapy and just being in that damn hospital bed and room for all those days and all those nights just went away while we were sitting there. Just evaporated. It was as if the months behind me hadn't happened. I could see that Tonio felt the same as I did even though we didn't say a word about it. We were just grateful. It was as if we had a reprieve, a time-out, as if God decided to give us some private time just for one another, finally. Tonio may have thought I was drinking cappuccino, but I was really drinking appreciation.

I guess everybody knows this, but it just takes being deprived of something to make you appreciate it. I'd been away from the most familiar things for so long that I couldn't get enough of them. The plain feel of being able to sit on a sofa. The way the front yard looked when I walked to the door and then how it looked when I saw it through the living room window. Two different yards, really. One in the open air. One through glass. I loved the way a fork felt in my hand. I loved my hands in dishwater. I loved the softness of my pillow, mine.

In a hospital something is happening all the time. You hear voices. You hear footsteps. You hear announcements on the loudspeaker. You hear sirens from emergency. You listen to people walking and talking in the hall outside your door. At home I was so happy to know that nothing was happening, that Tonio was in the same room with me or just a room away, that I could use my own bathroom. You'll think I'm crazy when I tell you this, but I got a lot of pleasure just getting myself a glass of cold water.

Of course, all this didn't happen on the first day. It happened over the first week. On that first day I just sat on the sofa and drank cappuccino with Tonio and let the feeling of being in a house of my own take over. I took everything in like a sponge, and I loved every minute of it. Later, Tonio's father came over. He never said a word. He just smiled that half-smile of his (it must run in the family) and looked at me with that faraway look in his eyes that older people get when what they're looking at is only half of what they are really seeing. The other half they'd never find the words to talk about, but I think it has something to do with everything they remember and that built-in fear they have for whatever might be ahead of them but which they try to keep in its place. It's hard to describe, but I know it when I see it. That really doesn't explain it, but whoever said that everything has to have an explanation?

I remember that first evening so clearly, Carolina. I can't remember much about the second or third or fourth evening, but the first one I remember minute by minute. I was more tired than I realized because at one point I didn't remember a thing. I must have gone out like a battery. At one minute I was talking to Tonio and his father and feeling the best I've ever felt, and then nothing. Tonio told me the next day that I fell asleep while I was talking to him. Right there on the sofa, sitting up. And I can't tell you anything else except that I woke up the next morning in bed under the sheets with that butter-scotch spread over me. Tonio told me that he just carried me in, somehow got me out of my clothes and into my nightgown and under the covers and then let me sleep and sleep. But now I'll tell you a little secret. He left the babushka on my head. He knew how sensitive I was about that. Wasn't that considerate? My hair hadn't really started to come back, and the top of my head was like a piece of soapstone, but he had enough—what's the word for it—care or whatever not to disturb anything even though I was asleep and wouldn't have known the difference anyway.

"YOUR hair is starting to grow back," said Carolina.

"But slowly. So s—l—o—w—l—y," said Halleluiah. "I look like one of those marine recruits from Pendleton."

"It's possible that it will come back fuller, stronger. Sometimes it happens that way."

"It will never grow where the scar is though, will it?"

"No."

"Why?"

"Because hair never grows out of scar tissue. There's nothing that can be done about that."

"I'll just comb my hair over the scar when it's long enough. There are all kinds of tricks."

"I'm a woman too, Lue, as well as a doctor. I know just how you feel about that, and I'd be thinking just like you if I were sitting where you're sitting."

Halleluiah smiled and joined her hands on her lap. "Carolina?"

"Yes."

"Do you believe in telling your patients the truth?"

"It depends."

"On what?"

"On who the patient is, on how much he or she can accept without being destroyed if the news is bad, on how much each individual patient can pull."

"Would you tell me the truth?"

"Yes," said Carolina, frowning. "Yes, I think I would. But if the news was bad, I would find it the hardest thing to do in my life."

"Have you told me the truth so far?"

"Yes."

"Honest to God?"

"Honest to God."

"I'm still not free and clear, am I?"

"No."

"When will I be?"

"I don't know the answer to that, Lue. Nobody does. We just have to keep a close watch. Regular check-ups. Just like today."

"And in the meanwhile?"

"Live. Live to the limit of your abilities."

"I don't even know my abilities now."

"Try. Your body will tell you what you can do."

"Does that include..."

"Yes?"

"You know. Making love. Tonio and I have never made love. When I was in the hospital, it wasn't in the script. You can't even think about lovemaking when you're nauseated half the time. But in the past week..."

"Just live, Lue. Don't cheat yourself."

"I'm the guilty party here, Carolina. Fear."

"It won't affect your condition one way or the other. Don't think so negatively."

"Are you sure it won't?"

"You asked me before if I told my patients the truth. Well, that's what I've just told you. The truth."

"There's something else that I want to ask you."

"Ask."

"Not now. I don't have the words for it now. It's not about me. It's about Tonio."

"Ask, Lue."

Halleluiah stood and walked to the window. It was raining. The rain pelted the window-glass so hard that she could not see through the thick smear of water. "If something happens to me... I mean if things don't work out, I don't want Tonio to be alone the rest of his life. I know him, Carolina. He's the kind of man who'd keep to himself if I weren't around any more. That's not good for anybody."

"Don't think that way, Lue."

"I can't help it. My whole life now is a question mark. How else can I think?"

"Think about today. Just today. That's really all that we all have anyway, isn't it?"

ONE thing this disease teaches you is fear. I'd never really been afraid of anything in my life. All during my teens I was a tomboy. I could ride a boy's bike, play football, ride on the fastest roller coaster, run like the wind. Never got a scratch, never broke a bone. I was never afraid to be alone either, Carolina. Never.

From the day I learned that I had this thing in my head, I started to change. It started to take over. It laid down all the rules, and it was playing for keeps. It changed the way I looked at everything. It changed the way I looked at death. I always thought death was a long way off. Old people died. Soldiers died. Foreigners died. That's what death used to mean to me. Suddenly the arrow pointed straight at me. I was the target, and I couldn't sidestep it.

I used to stay up nights wondering what it would be like to be dead. I would lie still with my hands at my sides, rehearsing. It was all so damn dumb, such a waste of time. How can you rehearse for what you don't know a thing about? But I kept trying to understand what death really meant, and all I came up with was trying to imagine the world without me. I couldn't do it. Nobody can really because we are the world. I mean the world is how we experience it. How can anybody take that experience out of his own life, take the world out of himself? You can't, right?

Well, I got over that phase. That was just before the chemo and the radiation started, and then I really knew what "sick" meant. My body wasn't me anymore. It turned against me. When I threw up, I couldn't stop myself, couldn't control it. I had the dry heaves. I'd sit on the toilet, and the sweat would pour off me, and at the same time I was cold as dry ice. There were days when I couldn't get out of bed. I remember one night when I just crawled into the bathroom and stayed there until they came to check on me. But while I was in the bathroom, I realized what fear really was. It's what you feel when you have no defenses or when your defenses don't mean a damn thing. I've said that before to you, but I can't improve on it. I knew then that I wasn't afraid of dying because there's no way you can be afraid of what no one knows anything about. The thought of it can bring you to a standstill, paralyze you, but that's not the same as fear. The fear I felt was really the fear of pain. Fear of being hurt and not being able to stop it. Fear of shrinking away to fifty or sixty pounds of meat and bones on a hospital bed with tubes sticking into every part of me. That terrified me so that I couldn't think. I just prayed. When they came to check on me in the bathroom, that's what I was doing—praying. After that I prayed myself to sleep on so many nights I lost track.

Fear short-circuits everything else, Carolina. I began to hate myself for being afraid. Then I began to hate that damn tumor that started all this in the first place. Little by little I felt my hate getting stronger and stronger until it was stronger than my fear. And when I reached that point, believe it or not, I was all right for a while. I was myself. Tension and counter tension. One canceled out the other. Or maybe one just kept the other from getting the upper hand. The problem is that it's not natural to keep that much hatred inside of yourself all the time. It eats you up. And finally. you turn into a shell or an old prune, and that lets the fear come to life again, and by then it's stronger than it was in the beginning. So, the whole fight starts again until you reach the right balance and try to keep it. But after a while you reach a point where you either stop struggling and just give up or you decide to keep up the old hate-fear fight for what's left of your life. That's what your life turns into—a wrestling match, and you can't quit or surrender even if you want to because mercy doesn't figure into this. Or maybe it's better to compare it to swimming. You swim and swim, and you can't rest. You'd love nothing better than to rest, but you can't because you'll drown the minute you try it.

There's no real pain to fight. It's not like the worst of headaches or anything like that. Of course, there was the nausea from the therapy, and that's hell on earth for as long as it lasts, but you know that it's going to pass, and that gives you hope. But otherwise, there's no pain, Carolina. And that makes everything so damn mysterious. You don't know where to focus your attention the way you do when you have a toothache or a burn. But when there's no pain, what can you do? You know you're involved with something that's lethal, but what is it? It scares you even more because you don't feel anything. It's almost like something that isn't real, but you know it is. And then another kind of fear starts, and it feeds on itself until it takes over.

I've heard so many stories about people who are really brave in situations like mine. But what's the point? Brave for what? When you're sick, you're sick. What does bravery have to do with that? In the beginning I tried to keep my courage up, especially when Tonio or Muz or Tonio's father was there. And I'm glad I did because when someone you love is up against it you feel it twice as bad as they do, and I knew they all loved me. But that wasn't the point. The main thing was learning to survive, working to survive, praying to survive.

ONCE in the bathroom Halleluiah removed her bathrobe. Then she slipped the babushka from her head and studied herself in the full-length mirror. Because she wanted to leave a viewing of her head until the end of her self-inspection, she began with her feet, then up her pale shanks to her knees, then to her thighs. She ran her hands over the soft skin of her thighs down to her calves that she had shaved earlier, and the skin felt firm and smooth as a healthy cheek. She looked at her hips and the way her thighs touched just below the brown tufts of hair that grew from either side of her groin inward to cover her small cleft. After that she appraised her breasts, noticing that the right one was, for some reason, slightly lower than the left. No one else would have noticed the millimeter of difference, but she did. She always had. It was always the first thing she noticed about herself, and it bothered her sense of the symmetry of things. One thing she did like was that her nipples were fronted on either breast and not at the nether ends so that they looked alert and not exhausted.

She would have preferred to stop at her shoulders rather than look higher. And she actually stopped there for several minutes before she looked at her face and head. She smiled at herself as if satisfied that her face was still hers. But the smile faded when she studied her scalp. The hair was sprouting somewhat unevenly, and the longest hairs were less than a half-inch high. She thought again of the marines from Pendleton, especially the new recruits on their first leave, and saw how much she resembled them. Male or female, it made no difference, she thought. The scar was still a pale red line bracketed at either tip with similar red lines, each line marking the edge of the flap that had been sliced and lifted out to make the removal of the tumor possible. She leaned forward slightly so that she had a clearer view of the scars. She tried to imagine how she would train her hair to cover the scars after it had grown back thick enough for her to comb it.

She had seen enough. She shut her eyelids tightly and released them only after she had turned toward the rapidly filling bathtub. She sprinkled several drops of gel that bloomed immediately into pink suds. Instantly the entire bathroom smelled of lilac.

Stepping into the tub, she felt she was not only in another element but in another time of her life, a younger time. The warm and sudsy water seemed to mother her when she sat and relaxed so that she felt protected. For some reason she let the faucet continue to run because she dreaded the silence that would happen as soon as she turned off the squared bronze taps. The jet of water from the faucet seemed to be keeping her company. She remembered what a priest once told her about water and baptism, and she suddenly understood the connection—the idea of cleanliness, renewal, refreshment.

For several minutes she tried to keep everything but her face underwater. When she was fully relaxed after doing that, she soaped herself perfunctorily and cleansed herself with the washrag. Then she unplugged the tub, stood up and stepped out on the bathmat to dry herself. She looked down at the draining bathwater now that she was out if it as so much waste.

After she sleeved herself into her bathrobe again, she started to arrange her headscarf to cover her scalp as she always did, then stopped. She waited, folded the scarf in thirds and squared it carefully on the dressing table beside the sink.

When she opened the bathroom door, she saw Tonio in his pajamas. He was sitting on his side of the bed with his back toward her.

"Tonio," she said.

"Yes, Lue," he answered, but he still did not turn around.

She walked around the bed until she was standing in front of him. He raised his eyes to her and smiled.

"I'll bet you never thought you'd be making love to a bald woman, did you?"

He smiled again, then dropped his gaze.

"Tonio," she said after a pause.

"Yes, honey."

"I may not look like much on the outside now, but inside I'm the same."

"SSShhhh."

"I had to say that."

"Not to me, Lue. I've known that all along."

She began to cry softly. She felt the tears dropping from her eyelids and down her cheeks, but she did not bother to stop them. "It just seems so damn unfair to me. Why did this have to happen to me... to us?"

He reached for her hands and held them before he stood slowly and put his arms around her shoulders, then her waist. She felt limp in his clasp, like someone in partial collapse or totally boneless. It gave Tonio the feeling that she would drop to the floor if he released her. Finally, when he knew the time of tears was over, he reached up with his right hand until he found her chin. He tilted her face up to his. She kept her eyelids shut, but the tear-paths, still moist but drying, were clearly visible—one a straight fall down the cheek, and the other an inexplicable meanderer that started straight and then detoured and stopped at her nostril.

He kissed each eye, then held her close to him. When they finally released one another, she walked to the other side of the bed, removed her bathrobe and eased herself under a single sheet. Tonio watched her. After a moment he turned off the lamp beside the bed and slipped under the sheet beside her. For several moments they were quiet and still before they turned simultaneously toward one another, somehow arranging their arms so that they were embracing side by side exactly as they had been embracing standing up.

"Why do I feel like something branded?" she asked.

"Put that out of your mind, Lue. This can happen to anybody any time. It's not like you brought it on yourself. There's no shame in it."

"Then why do I feel it?" She paused. "I remind myself of those women I've read about who had their heads shaved because they slept with Nazis."

"That's loco talk. Put that out of your head."

"Do you love me, Tonio?"

"Not a chance."

"Don't tease me, Tonio. I need to hear you tell me. Especially now."

He shifted so that her face tilted upward toward his. "What if I told you that I can't not love you, that it's like asking my eyes not to want to see or asking my heart not to want to beat? What if I told you that?"

"Just three words. That's enough."

"I. Love. You."

"You're everything to me, Tonio. If it weren't for you, I don't know how..."

He kissed her forehead, then the scar on her scalp. She kissed his cheek, then found his mouth and adjusted her lips to his and held the kiss until she had to pull back to breathe.

Tonio sat up in the dark and eased his legs over the side of the bed. He removed his pajama top, then slid down the bottoms over his knees and ankles to the floor and left them there.

"I don't know why I put those things on in the first place."

"Mr. Modesty."

"Mr. Modesty wants to lie back down next to you and resume."

"Be my guest."

She twisted slightly so that she was partly on her back and partly on her side. She opened her arms to his as he came close to her and held him for a moment as tightly as a drowning woman might fasten herself to her rescuer.

Tonio let his left leg slide between her thighs, felt her muscles tighten there and clamp his leg to her body as much out of instinct as will, loosened his arms so that she could turn on her back and then looked down at her through the darkness. He waited to hear her breathe or move, but there was nothing.

"Lue?"

"Yes."

"Are you all right?"

"Try me."

"You know what I mean. Are you?"

"Try me, Tonio."

She reached for his arm and drew him down to her. They kissed again and clung to one another without breaking the kiss as he lifted himself on top of her. She accepted him with an ease she never thought possible for the first time, and he entered her slowly and carefully as the right key might enter the right lock. They gripped and rocked together until their restraints vanished, and Halleluiah screamed not so much from the intensity of what she was feeling but from the surprise of it. Again, her body surprised her, achieving a pleasure that seemed until that moment beyond her.

During the entire act Tonio felt his passion for her tempered by caution so that he moved carefully on her and in her.

"Don't hold back," she whispered once to him. "I want it to happen."

Tonio was surprised when she moved with such vigor at her climax that he could not control his movements any longer, and the result was that her final spasms and his happened simultaneously. Afterward, they remained together, savoring the fading pleasure for as long as it lasted.

Lying later on their backs, side by side, they never said a word. It was like they were listening to music or the echo of music without the interruption of any intervening sound.

"Tonio..."

"Yes."

"Do you know when people say, 'This is it.'"

"Yes."

"Do you ever wonder what they mean?"

"I don't think they know."

"I know."

"Know what?"

"What 'it' is..."

"Tell me."

"Us. This. Here. Now."

"Do you really think so?" he said and laughed.

She turned on her side and faced him. "Yes, I think so." Then she caught a glimpse of his white teeth in the darkness. "Are you teasing me?"

"I wouldn't dream of it."

"Tonio..."

"Yes."

"Do you now what I'm going to do? I'm going to tickle you..." She reached across his chest, feeling his chest hair soft on her underarm. "I'm going to tickle you for saying that until you say uncle." She was suddenly all over him, tickling his sides, his underarms, the backs of his knees, his toes.

"Uncle!" he shouted, rolling on his side to protect himself.

"Louder!"

"Uncle! Uncle!"

"In Spanish!"

"Tío. Tío."

"There," she said, sitting back on her haunches and easing off. "There. That's more like it."

"I had my fingers crossed when I said it."

"What does that mean?"

"Where I come from, it means it didn't count..."

"Oh, you..." And again, she went at him until finally she stopped out of sheer tiredness. For a moment or two she sat statue-still in the middle of the bed. He turned, sat up and held her against him. He could not be sure, but he sensed that she was shivering.

"Tonio?"

"Yes."

"Do you know what happiness is?"

"For me it's when you don't hanker for a thing, when you're okay the way you are, just as you are."

"That's part of it. "

"That's the main part."

"I'd say it's when you want right now to go on and on and on and on..."

"But it can't."

"I know, but you want it to. That's the important part. That's how I feel. I want right now to go on for the rest of my life even though I know it can't. That's happiness."

I DON'T know if it's love that's made me more conscious of it or not, Carolina, but I'm convinced now that women are more aware of what's beautiful than men are. It's just the way we're made, I guess. It starts with our own looks, and it's not just vanity. I mean we want to look as good as we can. And then we want everything to look good too. I have a small window ledge in the bathroom here—just a plain ledge right above the commode. Everybody who goes to a bathroom goes there to use the commode or the sink. Nothing mysterious about that. But that ledge kept looking so damned ordinary to me that I went out and bought some artificial flowers to put on it. That made all the difference—a little touch like that. Beautiful fake flowers. That changed everything.

IT HAD been Carolina's suggestion that she and Tonio meet in the hospital cafeteria. She knew that Tonio wanted to know everything she knew about Halleluiah's prognosis, and she wanted to tell him without being interrupted.

"Tonio," she began, "we've known one another all our lives. I talk to you the way I'd talk to someone in my own family, no differently. But for a few minutes I'm going to talk to you as a doctor, just a doctor, about a patient. Lue is the patient. I want you to know that I love her the way I love you, the way you love her. But I'm going to try to put that to one side so I can talk to you without disguising a thing. I don't want to raise any false hopes, and I'm not going to be a prophet of doom. I'm just going to tell you where we've come from, where we are and what's ahead."

"I don't want you to hide anything from me."

"I won't. Even if I tried, I couldn't, Tonio. You know me too well for that." She paused. "Let's start from the beginning. What we know for sure is that

Lue had a malignant tumor, an astrocytoma in the left frontal lobe." From her jacket pocket she withdrew an artist's rendering of the human skull with the top of the skull sectioned into quadrants. She spread the drawing on the table between them. "Here, let me show you on this so you know what I'm talking about. Here. Here is the frontal lobe. This is where the tumor was. Any kind of tumor there, even a benign one, would have had unacceptable consequences. The fact that it was malignant made the whole situation much more serious. We follow a basic procedure in operations like this. The main thing we want the surgery to achieve is to remove the tumor—or as much of it as possible. Usually, we don't get it all no matter how hard we try. But we want to get the maximum so that the chemo and the radiation have that much less to deal with." She paused and put the drawing back in her jacket. "I think the operation was as good as we could hope for. And so far, she's responded well to the therapy. She's young and in good health, and that helps as well. We don't want any patient to be worse after the therapy than before it. But this is a lethal sickness. We can't be sentimental about it."

"How is she now? Right now?"

"I'd like nothing better to tell you, Tonio, than to say she's free and clear. I can't. None of us can. This is a disease where you can't ever drop your defenses. But with Lue, so far, so good. We'll continue to monitor the results indefinitely. And that's really all I can tell you."

"That's everything? There's nothing you're hiding?"

"No, I'm not hiding anything. In fact, the prospects seem better now than they seemed a week or so ago."

"How?"

"Well, she's home now, and she's happier at home. I can see that. No one likes to stay in a hospital. Being home is the best therapy in the world for her. You can't underestimate the effect of this on her. Spiritually, I mean. Psychologically." She paused. "One of my patients wrote me the other day, and there's something in her letter I want you to hear." She removed a folded letter form her jacket, opened it and began to read, "'Survivors cross a river once they have gone though the cancer experience; they can never go back.' That's important for you to know, Tonio. I think you have to prepare yourself for a change in Lue. Maybe a permanent change. Sometimes in some cases there is a change in personality itself. We have no way of predicting what will happen or guarding against it. The best medicine is what she'll get from you. Attention. Affection. There can never be too much of that. Apart from hope, that's the only life-line a patient has. It's the only thing sometimes between them and despair. Despair is the real cancer. Once patients contract that it's only a matter of time before you see the bad effects. They start to die from within. In fact, once despair gets them in its grip the patients are as good as dead. There just remains the formality of a burial later. I don't think Lue is the kind of person who is given to despair, but we—you—have to keep her spirits up. It's the most important thing. In my opinion it's a better therapy than all the medicine on earth. We can't explain why, but it is."

THE woman who owned the place—at least she acted like she owned the place—was wearing one although I found out later that she didn't need it. Advertising, I suppose. You know, the way the girl at the perfume counter wears the store's cologne to show she believes in it.

She led me into a showroom where all the heads were and said, "All right, my dear, meet the wigs." There must have been fifty heads on shelves all around the room, and each head had a different wig on it. Black, brown, a dozen flavors of blonde, a dozen and a half dozen flavors of gray, white, purple or close to it and then some other colors I didn't have a name for, I swear.

The owner was a wee bit of a woman. I mean wee as in short. But she was wide as a baseball catcher. And she kept talking so much that I felt like cutting out, but I didn't. She kept telling me that a big part of her business was because of the demand created by women "in my situation." I'd leveled with her about that in the beginning. She said if it weren't for women with my problem and for black women, the store would have gone bankrupt months before. "It's all a matter of image, my dear," she said. "It's how women think they want to be seen when they're in public. That way you're no different that the rest, so just relax."

What can you tell a woman like that? Maybe she was dead right, but just then I didn't want to hear about image and all that stuff. It was just plain vanity. Why not say it straight out? And maybe there was even a little shame in it. I just wanted to go outside my own house with hair on my head and not a piece of cloth. I'd read all that stuff about a woman's crowning glory being her hair, and I'd always made light of it. What did I know then? I had all the hair I needed when I thought that way. But when you lose your hair like me, all at once, that's when you appreciate what crowning glory means.

I just walked around the showroom and looked at all those samples of crowning glory on all those shelves. She asked me if I wanted a wig that matched the color of my real hair when I had hair or if I wanted a change. She picked up Miss Purple when she said that. She saw in a flash that I wasn't interested, so she went conservative. I just let her talk and went shopping around on my own. I asked her where all this hair came from, and she told me from women. There were all kinds of sources—in the orient, in Latin America, all over. It's really quite an industry.

Finally, I found a head with a wig on it that rhymed with my hair in the days before the chemo took it away. I was a kind of dark blonde when I was a teenager, but in my early twenties my hair got naturally darker until it was the same color as a brown crayon. But my hair was always very fine. I had a lot of it, but it didn't have much body. I just ran my fingers over the wig on this one head, and it felt like my hair used to feel, and it was close to the same color. I lifted the wig off and turned it around and around in my hand.

"You can't tell a thing until you try it on, dear," the owner said. "There are some dressing rooms right behind you. Just take the wig in and try it on. In private. Just put it on like a cap and work it around until you have it the way you want it."

I took the wig and checked into one of the dressing rooms. The lights there were like sunlamps. Too bright. They revealed too damn much, if you know what I mean. Finally, I had the courage to take the scarf from around my head and look at myself under the full glare—Miss Plucked Chicken from California. It didn't matter that I knew what I was going to see in that mirror. It was just that something in me always kept hoping that this whole business was nothing but a bad dream and that one day I would wake up and realize it. It's human nature, I suppose. You told me once that most of your patients were that way—rejecting and rejecting what they couldn't bring themselves to accept. Why is that? Why can't we just accept and go on? Animals do. Birds do. But not us, no sirree.

After I had my fill of bald me in the mirror, I got around to putting this "hairpiece" on my head. The owner was right. It was like putting on a cap, a loose cap. The damn thing kept shifting all over my head like an omelet—first too far back, then over the right ear, then over the left, then down too far in front of me so I looked like Betty Boop. Finally, I worked it to where I wanted it and frizzed it up here and there until I started to look like me, myself and I, the real me that I remembered. To be honest about it I think I even looked a little better than the me I used to be, or maybe I just thought so. I don't know. After you've looked like someone scalped by an Apache, anything is an improvement. I stood in front of that dressing room mirror for almost five full minutes, just primping and adjusting and trying to get used to having a cap of some other woman's hair on my head. After all that I decided it was time to step out and face the public, so out I walked, and there was Mrs. Baseball Catcher waiting the way a woman waits for another woman to come out of the bathroom when she's been in line to use it and is in a hurry, if you get my meaning. I almost felt that she'd been timing me in there with a stopwatch.

"Dear, it's absolutely you. Honest to Betsy. It's you all over. You look totally stunning."

I told her I wasn't out to look stunning, just to look un-bald. By then there were a few other women in the showroom, and I didn't want to get into a give-and-take with a woman who didn't know how to whisper, so I thought I'd just finish the deal right then and there. When I handed her my credit card, she said, "You better get two hairpieces, honey. You won't regret it, believe me." I thought she was trying to corner me into a bigger sale, and she knew I was thinking what I was thinking because she said right away, "It's no matter to me if you get one or two, honey. Honest to God. I don't get paid commission. But you're going to need two, take it from me. You wouldn't guess it, but I went through something like you're going through. It's been five years next month, knock on wood. A breast. This one. I lost my breast, my hair, the whole nine yards. I had to buy what you're buying right now. I figured one hairpiece was enough. Why invest? It's just temporary. That's what I told myself.

Besides, hairpieces aren't cheap. I couldn't afford twins. But the saleswoman explained to me that two is the answer. You wash one, you wear one, she says. You get chewing gum or something in one, and you have a spare. You have some security, some back-up, she says. And she was right. So, I'm telling you what she told me, dear. I listened to her, and I'm glad I did."

She convinced me. I bought the identical twin of number one, watched her put them both in a hatbox together with a page of instructions about how to take care of the things, put that old scarf around my noggin and left. But it was two full days before I had the courage to let Tonio see me in one of them.

HE MAINTAINED a speed of fifty-five miles per hour all the way from Los Angeles to San Juan Capistrano. Halleluiah had not been in a car for a long drive for many weeks, and Tonio thought that a steady speed would be more reassuring to her than going at top speed just to get there. He watched her occasionally from the corner of his right eye. Rather than look at the road, she concentrated on the sky or the ocean on her right or the inland mountains on her left. Nothing that was not natural seemed to attract or interest her, he noticed. The highway, the other cars, the buildings on the roadsides and the passing towns might just as well have been invisible.

"Will Father Sanchez be there?" she asked.

"He told me he's been re-assigned to our parish again."

"We won't see him then?"

"Yes, we will. He doesn't leave until next week. I called him at the mission and told him we were coming."

She turned her head and stared at the ocean. “It’s always puzzled me to see how the ocean changes colors. There’s every shade of blue, and then there’s a belt of dark green, then a belt of black and then blue again.”

“It all has to do with the sky, they tell me. The water just reflects what’s above it. The sea’s not supposed to have any color by itself. It just takes on the colors it reflects. That’s the theory, but I can’t say I understand it.”

“What on earth is there in the sky right now that’s green?”

“Don’t you see all those green clouds up there, Lue?”

“Tonio, be serious. I want to learn.”

For the rest of the drive she continued to look at the ocean, smiling occasionally to herself and even humming to herself now and then as if looking at the ocean from a moving car were the most satisfying experience anybody could have. By the time they arrived at San Juan Capistrano, it was almost noon. The entrance to the shrine was crowded with tourists and pilgrims, but Tonio avoided them by using a side gate that led directly to the priests' house. Before entering the house, Tonio looked across the large courtyard to the chapel and an adjacent shop that sold the gimcrackery that he loathed: medals, ornate rosaries, bottles of blest water, carved statuettes. For Tonio this commercialization spoiled everything he associated with the shrine—its magnetism and its history as a devotional center. And besides, this mission contained, as he explained carefully to Halleluiah, the oldest building in California.

Father Sanchez was walking in the portico, and he smiled and shut his breviary as Tonio and Halleluiah approached him. Halleluiah could not help but notice how much he resembled Tonio. In some ways, she thought, they could pass as brothers. Both had the same undisguised smile, the sheer cheeks, the straight black hair, the priest's more abundant than Tonio's but exactly the same India ink color.

"Well," said Father Sanchez, making a point of greeting Halleluiah first. "The patient looks much better than the rest of us, don't you think so, Tonio?"

"Don't look too close, Father," she said, blushing and touching the new wig that she felt was not sitting properly on her head.

The priest and Tonio exchanged an abrazo and talked briefly and quietly in Spanish.

"Tonio explained to me that St. Peregrine has been your good protector so far, Lue," said Father Sanchez.

"So far," said Halleluiah.

The priest smiled and shrugged as if to say that "life" and "so far" were actually synonymous and that human beings should expect no more than that.

"I never really saw the chapel here," said Halleluiah. "I'd love to see it just to say I did."

"It's not what the French call 'nouveau'," said Father Sanchez.

"He's preparing you," said Tonio. "The chapel is one of the oldest buildings here. You'll see. It's narrow as an aisle and very small. And there are candles and candles and candles."

"I'd still love to see it," she said.

A group of tourists was just exiting the chapel when they entered. A young woman in their midst was talking authoritatively but almost disembodiedly about St. Peregrine as the patron of those stricken with cancer and then digressing to the Capistrano legend about the swallows and their annual departure and return along the adjacent coast.

The first scent that Hallelujah detected was the smell of melting candle-wax and the somehow holy aroma of wicks. As Tonio had told her, the chapel was long and with a single central aisle separating two sections of pews from another century—dark upright benches with wooden kneelers affixed to their backs so that the worshippers were compelled to kneel at attention flush against the backs of the pews in front of them and so forth from the rear to the front of the chapel. At the rear were bowers of pencil-slender candles in red glass candle holders, each candle of a different length depending upon when it had been lighted. In the center of each bower was a slotted metal box marked: OFFERINGS. To the left of each bower was a confessional, the curtains drawn back and tied with a sash, the seats and kneeler of priest and penitent respectively, vacant.

When Halleluiah looked down at the floor, she noticed that she was standing on a well-walked-on waffling linoleum, uneven and lumpy from the comings and goings of thousands.

After she looked at the compact, but overly decorated altar, Halleluiah was distracted by a shrine to Our Lady of Guadalupe to her left. Several candles were casting fire shadows across the face of the Virgin, and the entire replica looked ruddy and dark from having been in the rising path of candle smoke over many years. Halleluiah had seen the actual Virgin of Guadalupe in photographs and on postcards, and she saw that the face of the replica was essentially the same as the real portrait, only miniaturized.

"Have you ever been to Guadalupe, Tonio?' asked the priest.

"Just once."

"I should go again myself, but somehow I just don't make an opportunity. I should though. I should go." He turned to Halleluiah. "Have you ever gone, Lue?"

"No, but I've seen pictures, and I've read about it."

"It's important for us, I think. I mean for Catholics, not just Mexicans. We don't have true shrines in this hemisphere. Just Guadalupe." He paused. "Personally, I'm not an advocate of pilgrimages. I don't say so publicly, you understand. I can't do that. I don't want to disturb anybody's faith, and miracles, after all, can happen, and they do happen. But all the side-businesses that spring up around these shrines cheapen everything. I was in the Holy Land last year, and it was the same. Souvenirs, junk, the same." He nodded his head disapprovingly in the direction of the shop opposite the chapel.

"You just have to look through that stuff," said Tonio. "People commercialize everything. You have to know what to ignore."

"I agree with that," said Halleluiah.

"I suppose I do too, really," said the priest.

"It would have been nice if you could have married us here, Father," she said.

"It would have been nice, but it was impossible even if we had the time then, and we really didn't have the time. You'll notice all the renovation. The portico was just re-opened two days ago. Let me show you what they did."

He led her out of the chapel. He turned to Tonio, who was still standing just inside the doorway. "Come with us, Tonio," he said. "They've done some amazing things with the foundations here."

"In a minute. I just want to let Lue talk to somebody else besides me for a while. Go ahead. I'll catch up." He smiled and winked.

Father Sanchez and Halleluiah re-entered the portico that made three legs of a rectangle around the courtyard. He pointed to the Stations of the

Cross hooked into the portico walls at regular intervals and explained to her how they had been cleaned and spackled.

"Tell me," said Father Sanchez after they passed the last station. "How are you? Really."

"Minute by minute. Day by day. That's going to be my life from now on."

"Are your spirits good?"

"How can anybody be depressed around Tonio?"

"He loves you in a very special way. You know that, of course."

"Yes, I know that."

"I have a confession to make to you, Lue."

"You to me? I thought it worked the other way around."

"Not this time." He paused. He turned so that he was not fully facing her. "Tonio and I had a long talk just before your wedding. I... I wasn't very encouraging. To tell you the truth, I told him I thought he should wait until after the operation."

"Don't feel guilty about that. I told him the same thing."

"I thought first that he was going through with it —I have to tell you this—out of sympathy or pity—something like that, but I was absolutely wrong, believe me." He paused again and smiled at two tourists who were just passing him at that moment. When they were out of earshot he added, "By the time Tonio and I finished talking, I had to take back everything I was thinking before. I knew that he was doing the right thing, the only thing."

"You don't know how much I needed to hear that, Father. I knew it in my heart, but I needed to hear someone confirm it."

"Well, it's not something I'm telling you just for this occasion, Lue, something to make you feel good. It's much deeper than that. After Tonio and I finished talking that day, I came away with one definite impression—that your life meant as much to him as his own. I haven't changed my mind. Your life still means as much to him as his own, even more than his own. You—how can I say this?—you complete him. There's only you for him, no one else. That's why he saw no reason to wait. And he told me that he would never change. Besides, he thought it would make you stronger for what was ahead of you. Ahead of both of you."

"If it weren't for Tonio, Father, I wouldn't be here now. I wouldn't have anyone to survive for."

A group of men and women, obviously Mexican, were passing them, and one of the men stopped and spoke to Father Sanchez in Spanish.

"A la derecha," said the priest, pointing, and the man smiled and led the group in that direction.

"Ten to one they were looking for the rest rooms," said Halleluiah and smiled.

"Not this time, but it's happened, I assure you. No, they were looking for the chapel. The man said they were from Guadalajara. This mission means lot to Mexican people. It's like something that they feel belongs to them because of Junipero Serra. It's like something in the family, and they want to see the replica of the Virgin we have in the chapel. They're not here as tourists. They're here to pray. It's a matter of respect for them. There's a difference."

"I can understand that."

"You see that same faith at the real shrine in Guadalupe. The same spirit. There's no pretense about it. Just devotion... Of course, here they worship differently, but inwardly there's no difference."

"What do you mean?"

"Well, there's a large plaza outside of the church in Guadalupe. At any hour of the day or night you see Indians or people from the provinces crossing the plaza to the church on their knees. It's not done so much as a penance as out of—you'll understand this—love. You have the impression that these people could not imagine their lives without this devotion. It's something they would die for, I'm sure of it."

"The Indians do this?"

"Indians and Mexicans. There's an overlap. Besides, to be a true Mexican there should be some Indian blood in you."

"On their knees?"

"All the way on their knees. And the plaza is as long as a modern city block or more."

"I've read about that kind of praying in Ireland and some places in Europe and the Middle East, but I didn't think it existed here. I've never even seen a picture of it."

"Photographers don't take pictures. It's regarded as demeaning."

While talking, they had returned to the chapel entrance where the group of Mexican men and women were just exiting, each one blessing himself or herself in the Latin way, making the sign of the cross after skimming the holy water font but concluding by bringing the thumbnail of their right hand to their lips and kissing it as if that gave the act its proper signature.

"I wonder what happened to Tonio," Halleluiah said.

She entered the chapel with the priest. Two women in black shawls were sitting in one of the back pews. There was no one else. Then she saw Tonio. He was on his knees, two-thirds of the way up the central aisle. Father Sanchez saw him at the same time. He looked quickly at Halleluiah and gestured for her to leave with him.

When they were outside, he said, "I don't have to tell you why he's doing that..."

"No," she said and sat down on a bench beside the door and turned her face away from him.

"You shouldn't be upset," he said, touching her shoulder.

"I'm not upset, Father," she answered. She felt she was going to cry, and she was determined not to. "Honestly, I'm not upset. It's just..."

"You don't have to explain, Lue."

"It's just that..." She realized that she was crying, regardless. She couldn't stop herself. It was as if her eyes were just receiving the overflow of whatever feelings she was trying to find words for—as if the feelings were separate from the words and turned into tears as the only worthy way of releasing themselves. "It's only that..." She stopped and looked directly at Father Sanchez, ignoring completely the tears that had already reached her chin and were dropping on her blouse. "It's just that I never had anyone do anything like that for me before. Never in my whole life."

THE drive back to Los Angeles from the shrine was like a dream for me, Carolina. I pretended I was tired and even closed my eyes so Tonio would think I was asleep, but all the time I was more awake and alive than I've ever been in my whole life. I kept seeing him on his knees all the way up that aisle. And he was doing it for me. For my life. Well, I'll tell you, you can't ask anything more than that, can you? Tell the truth. Can you?

We might as well have been driving on the moon. I didn't hear any of the cars passing. I didn't even hear the radio that Tonio had on real low. You guessed it. A Dodger game. I was in another world. No, not another world. I was in the only world that mattered for me. It's a world where you know you're loved just for who you are and that nothing else really matters. If I died at that minute, I think I would have died the happiest woman in the world. Of course, dying wouldn't have interested me much right then. I was so full of life that I could barely contain myself, and all I wanted to do was live with that feeling forever. And beyond forever.

But little by little reality started to come back. I still had that damn wig on my head. And Tonio, by the way, had never said a word about it. I'd worn it without telling him in advance, but he never said a thing. I'm sure he saw it. He notices everything. But not a word one way or the other.

AFTER she had situated it exactly as she wanted it on her head and combed it carefully so that the hair no longer looked flattened, she pulled it off and threw it on the floor. She heard Tonio start the automatic dishwasher in the kitchen. She had wanted to put on the wig before dinner but had remained in the babushka. Even though she had worn the wig twice, once in the house and the second time on the trip to San Juan Capistrano, Tonio had yet to comment on it. Not that she wanted to talk about it. The less talk about "her situation" the better, she thought. Besides, she told herself, there ware thousands of other things to talk about, and she'd be damned if the surgery and the therapy and all the consequences and side effects were going to preempt a discussion of anything else. What else could be said about it? The subject exhausted itself quickly, and then there was nothing to do but repeat what you already knew.

"Lue," Tonio called from the kitchen.

"Yes."

"Do you want to finish your coffee?"

"I'll be in for it. Just give me a minute."

"We still have one chapter to go."

They were reading John Steinbeck's TORTILLA FLAT, or rather she was reading it to him. Her reading aloud was something Tonio had suggested in the hospital. He had brought a copy of Steinbeck's short stories, and he persuaded her to read one story a day. And she did. During her last week in the hospital, she had started reading TORTILLA FLAT. Tonio had personally chosen it, telling her it was one of his favorite books.

"Why do you like Steinbeck?" she had asked him.

"He's clear. And he understands people I know something about. And he understands justice. Or I should say he understands injustice, which is really saying the same thing in a different way. And that's what I look for every day of my life. Truth in what I read or hear. Justice where I live and work. Those are the main things."

She picked up the wig and donned it again, going through the same ritual of adjustments, combings, centerings, fluffings and compressings until it seemed to fit her like a football helmet. Even after she finished primping, she delayed going into the kitchen for several minutes until she was assured that she was wearing the wig, and not the wig her. She picked up TORTILLA FLAT and opened it to the page where she had stopped reading the night before. Halleluiah sat at the kitchen table, holding the book, and waited for Tonio to notice her. When he did look at her, he did not change his expression at all. It was as if he saw nothing different about her.

"I marked the place in the book where you stopped," he said.

She picked up the book and set it down again. "Tonio?"

"Yes."

"Does it look that ridiculous?"

"What?"

"You know what."

He stood and walked slowly toward her and kissed her first on the tip of her nose and then on her mouth.

"That's not an answer," she said.

"Yes, it is. My kind of an answer."

"But I need you to tell me if it looks natural or not. I hate phoniness, and this feels so phony I could scream."

"That means you want an opinion, not an answer."

"What's the difference?"

"The difference is that my answer was the real answer, that everything is the same to me, operation or no operation, wig or no wig..."

"But you didn't even notice. I had to ask you. I've been waiting for three days for you to notice."

"I noticed."

"Why didn't you say something then?"

"Didn't my not saying anything say something to you?"

"What?"

"That it didn't matter. That I'd love you the same no matter what you had on your head. You could have a bushel basket on your..." He kissed her again before he finished the sentence.

"Tonio," she whispered after the kiss ended.

"A sus ordines. At your orders..."

"I'm sorry."

"No need to be sorry."

"But I do need your opinion. I'm a woman, Tonio. I can't ignore appearances completely. And I'm self-conscious about this thing. So, tell me."

He stepped back and studied her as if he were studying a painting. "Well," he said finally. "It's a very good match."

"Match for what?"

"If I didn't know better, I couldn't tell the difference between the way you are now and the way you were."

"Honest?"

"Honest."

YOU KNOW what happiness is, Carolina? It's wanting what you feel right now to go on and on and on even though you know it can't. If you think that happiness is somewhere in the future and not now, you're totally wrong. That just means you're unhappy and want things to change. When I'm with Tonio, I just want everything to stay that way. Now that I have this problem in my body, I want it even more. I look around and wonder how many people feel the way I do. I know one man who fell in love with a girl in Japan when he was stationed there. She could only speak Japanese, but he told me that he felt what she meant even though he didn't understand a word in Japanese. He married her over there and brought her back, and she learned English and the rest, but that didn't seem to make any difference. It's what they had at the start that stayed with them. And I know another girl who married someone her mother didn't approve of. But she was sure of what she felt. When someone reminded her of how her mother felt, she just said, "I'm not marrying my mother." And the marriage was still working, last I heard. Of course, there are a lot of train wrecks. Some happen early, and some happen late, but they happen. I know of one girl who married when her husband was still in medical school. She worked and helped him finish. He became a plastic surgeon, and they had two children. I don't know what happened, but they reached a point when he didn't even speak to her for a whole year though they lived in the same house. He was making a lot of money. One day he just went off with one of his patients. Who knows what happened? Plastic surgeons can be good catches for some women—especially women with a little money and a feeling that they need a little updating here and there.

I've given up figuring out what keeps couples together or breaks them up. Some say you can fall out of love as quickly as you can fall into it. I don't know if I'll live long enough to find out. I hope I never do.

HALLELUIAH wondered why she was watching them even as she watched them. For three successive nights the same scene had evolved before her very eyes while she stood at the kitchen window, readying the dishes for the dishwasher. The kitchen window permitted her to look across a crevice to the fifth and sixth floors of an apartment building that faced the back yard. It was the rear of the apartment building that she saw—tier after tier of back porches, some shaded by yellow awnings, some adorned with yucca plants or flower boxes of impatiens or phlox.

What Halleluiah had seen for two successive nights happened in two apartments, one directly above the other. On the first night in an apartment on the fifth floor she watched a gray-haired man busying himself in the kitchen. She could not tell whether he was cooking or setting a table for dinner or both, but it was clear to her that he was doing whatever he was doing alone. After several moments she saw a woman enter the kitchen. She was wearing a white dressing gown and was trying to be cheerful while walking unsteadily toward the kitchen table. Halleluiah noticed that she was using a tripod cane and that she was relying on it heavily. The man stood ready to help her if necessary, but it was obvious that help was not what the woman wanted unless she had no choice in the matter. Still the man hovered near her, his arms poised to catch or guide but not actually touching her. When the woman finally reached her chair, she stood satisfyingly erect for a moment and smiled at the man to show that she had made it on her own. Then the man pulled out her chair for her, and she sat down. Then he disappeared from Halleluiah's view and returned with a tureen in his hands and set it down carefully in the middle of the table. Then he lighted two candles at either end of the tureen, turned down the kitchen lights and took his chair opposite the woman. Then they bowed their heads, and Halleluiah realized that they were saying their grace. That's when she looked away because she felt at that point that she was prying. Later that night she thought again and again of that scene in the kitchen... the man making a special dinner for his crippled wife, the two of them sitting with their heads bowed at the table, the twin candles like vigil lights burning softly between them.

What Halleluiah saw in the apartment above on the following night was what she didn't want to see. She had observed the woman in that apartment on several occasions performing the same back-porch ritual. She was a small woman with defiant blonde hair teased as if it had been permanently affected by static electricity, and she came out onto the balcony daily to water a box of peonies there. On this particular night there was a man on the balcony, a chest-heavy man with rolled-up white shirtsleeves. He sat scanning a newspaper and paid no attention to the woman who was watering the flowers behind him. The woman was wearing a yellow dress. After she finished watering the flowers, she stood beside the man as if waiting for him to take notice of her. The man concentrated on the newspaper and did not look up. The woman's reaction was to walk provocatively in front of the man, but the man's concentration on the newspaper did not break. When it became apparent to her that all her attempts to get his attention were useless, she spun on her heel and marched through the kitchen and out of sight. Still the man did not stir. He just concentrated on the open page in front of him. Each time he finished one page, he slowly turned to the next, and then the next, and then the next. Except for the movement of his arms in turning the pages, he appeared to Halleluiah as if he were a seated statue. After ten minutes the woman returned. Except for her pink underpants, she was naked. She had removed the dress in the interval and was standing in the doorway with the dress wadded under her arm. After a moment she began speaking to the man. At one point she held the dress in her right hand and shook it in the man's face. Slowly, almost too slowly, the man folded the paper in half, then in half again and set it aside. Then in one quick movement he seized the dress and flung it over the balcony railing. The woman lunged toward the railing to grasp it, but it was already out of reach. She turned on the man, but at the very same moment he struck her with his open hand across the side of her head. The woman put up her hands as if to ward off a second blow, but it was too late. The second one landed on the same spot, and it threw her to the floor. While she lay there, her feet drawn up and her arms shielding her breasts, the man picked up the newspaper, and walked slowly through the kitchen and into the interior of the apartment. For several moments the woman remained curled on the porch floor. Then she drew herself to her feet, somewhat uncertainly. She made her way into the kitchen and leaned against the sink. Halleluiah watched as she filled a small pitcher with water and returned to the porch where she began watering the peonies. When she finished, she sat in the chair the man had been sitting in, covered her face with her hands and began to sob into them. It was at that second that Halleluiah heard Tonio return from the pharmacy where he had gone to purchase a prescription for her. She turned from the scene in the apartment and stood still for a moment. She found herself shivering like someone who has stood in a cold wind longer than planned.

"I bought some chocolate kisses at the pharmacy," Tonio was saying. "I just felt like eating that kind of chocolate... "

She was in his arms before he could finish the sentence. She pressed herself against him, then kissed him so desperately that he almost lost his balance.

"I think I'll go to the drugstore more often," he said, laughing and swaying with her. After a moment he added seriously, "Is anything wrong? Are you all right?" He put his hand under her chin and tried to lift her face to his. He could feel tears on his finger backs. "What's wrong, Lue?"

"Nothing."

"Then why the tears?"

"I'm happy, that's all. She waited. "Don't say anything, Tonio. And don't look at me, please. Just hold me and let me hold you like this for a couple of minutes. Okay?"

"Okay."

I THINK the worst time for me, Carolina, was when I had that setback or whatever it was. I felt I was on the mend. I'd gotten used to my reliable old wig—both of them—and gone for walks and met some of the neighbors and all that. I was just starting to enjoy being domestic, and I was going public, little by little. Along the way I had my share of dark thoughts—you just can't help that—about how it would be if the doctors hadn't gotten the whole tumor, but I tried to keep those thoughts where they belonged. Dead and nailed down. Give them an inch, and they eat you alive. If you just think of the worst that can happen, you end up paralyzed. You've got to think that you're going to live forever. And the funny thing is that that's the way most people think anyway. You can't really live unless you believe you're going to live forever, right?

Anyway, on this day Tonio was at work, and I had just finished lunch by myself. I was siting in the living room. I wasn't reading or watching television or doing anything except being in my own living room and appreciating the dickens out of that. Suddenly my left arm felt like your arm feels when it goes to sleep or when you bang your crazy bone against something hard and, until the feeling comes back into your elbow, it might as well belong to someone in the next county. For a minute I didn't pay any attention to it, but it didn't go away. Then I had the same feeling in my left leg—like pins, thousands of little pins doing a job on me there. I started to talk to myself. "Come on, Halleluiah. Stay calm, old girl. It's just a passing thing. Just stay calm. Steady and calm." Honest to God, I was afraid to move. I was even afraid to blink. I mean I was afraid to find out that I might not be able to move or blink. I thought of standing up, but as soon as I put a little weight on my left foot, I knew that I'd fall over if I kept going, that Mr. Foot wouldn't hold me up. And that's when the real terror took over. It's like the terror you feel in a dream when you're sinking in mud or when the fire starts at your feet and begins to climb up and up, and you can't move. You can't scream. You try, but nothing happens.

The phone was over on the other side of the room. I figured I could get to it if I was able to slide over, but I decided that it might be better to wait and see if my arm and my leg decided to join the rest of me. I thought maybe I'd sing along just to keep my spirits up, but whatever was making my arm and leg numb was doing a job on my voice too. My voice sounded like an old man's voice. I was having a hard time getting my lips to make words. I thought I'd be all right with the national anthem, but I never got to the first line. God, I was scared out of my teeth. All I could think of was that I was coming apart, coming totally apart, and I couldn't stop it. And I couldn't call anybody or do anything about it.

I must have sat there all afternoon. I even went to the bathroom on that chair, Carolina. Just water. But I couldn't hold it any more. It just came out of me without my having any say in it one way or the other. That's when I started to cry. Brave me. I just sat there like a kid who's peed all over herself, and I cried like it was the end of the world. You do the craziest things when you're scared to death, believe me. But then it passed. I got so calm that I thought I'd died and gone to heaven, but just then in came Tonio. For a minute he didn't understand. But then he sensed something was off-center, and he ran over to me. He looked right into my eyes, and I tried to talk, but my tongue felt like a rubber ball in my mouth by then. He saw how wet I was and how wet the chair was and all, and the next thing I knew he had me in his arms and was carrying me out the door and into the car, and then we were heading back to the city like a police car in a chase.

It was the same hospital. I knew that in a minute. It made me feel that the game was up as soon as we pulled into the emergency entrance. I beat against the inside of the door with my right hand, but so what? Beat by beat, just like a loser. I was still beating the door when Tonio opened it, and he and another guy lifted me out and onto a gurney and off we went. Tonio stayed with me, telling me that he wouldn't leave no matter what and not to worry about a thing, everything was going to smooth out, all nice things. I was scared so much by then that I ate up whatever he was telling me without thinking about it. It was the tone of his voice. I needed something, and that was it. That kept me from going bonkers, honest. I felt so helpless. I didn't know what was wrong, but I knew something was wrong, that's for sure. I didn't know where I was heading. And hospitals give me the creeps anyway.

Once they had me in a private room in an actual bed, I felt a little better. Then you came in, Carolina. I saw you smile at me, but it was just a face-smile. It didn't go any deeper. I knew then that something was the matter with me, and no kidding. I reached for your hand, remember? And sure as Sunday, I did it with my left hand. My left hand was working again. It came back to life when I wasn't looking. The tingling was all gone, and I didn't have that tingling feeling in my leg anymore either. That's when I pulled your face down to mine, remember, until our cheeks were touching, and we cried together there like two sisters.

Later you gave me something to make me sleep, and whatever it was worked like a charm. I slept into the middle of the next day. You were smiling your real smile then, and you gave me a few more tests and kept me one more day for good measure. By the third night I slept in my own bed. Remember when we talked, honey? It was our best talk, and I made you promise, and you did.

CAROLINA returned to her office where Tonio was waiting for her. He had the look of a man about to receive a sentence he dreaded but would be unable to avoid.

"Don't look that way, Tonio," said Carolina. "I expected a relapse like this at some point. In fact, I thought it might happen even sooner."

"How is she?"

"By now she's probably asleep. I'll check her again tomorrow, and I may even discharge her the day after that if everything remains stable."

Tonio seemed relieved to hear that, but he still looked at her questioningly.

"Why do you always look at me that way when I answer what you ask me?"

"Because I know you are not telling me everything." Tonio walked toward her, kissed her on the cheek and left the office.

Carolina slid into her chair behind her desk, leaned forward briefly on her elbows and let her head fall forward on her crossed arms. She did not want to sleep. It was just that suddenly her head seemed to have gotten too heavy to support. Remembering Tonio's exit, she told herself that she had tried to be convincing. What kept coming to the fore of her thinking time and time again was the result of the CAT scan, which had shown her that the tumor had begun to grow again, that the operation had not completely cauterized it and that the subsequent therapy had only kept it at bay, not erased it. She had shown the CAT scan to two other doctors. Both confirmed her worst suspicions. She had wondered how she would face Halleluiah or Tonio. Should she conceal what she knew or be absolutely frank? Should she only tell them the minimum?

"I'm not asleep," Halleluiah said when Carolina returned to her room.

"You will be. I want you to rest now."

"Is Tonio here?"

"He was. I told him he could leave. It took quite a bit of convincing."

After a pause Halleluiah said, "Are you still here, Carolina?"

"Yes, Lue."

"Come over so I can see you."

Carolina stepped closer to the bed and leaned over. She smiled and waited until Halleluiah smiled back.

"It's so good to see an unprofessional face," Halleluiah said. "When they took me up for the scan, I didn't recognize a soul."

"How are you?"

"Tired."

"You'll sleep soon. It'll do you good. Tomorrow everything will be better. You'll see."

"Carolina?"

"Yes."

"How am I doing?"

"Good. You had a little setback, but I expected it, and I think we can deal with it."

"Carolina?"

"Yes."

"When you don't answer me head-on, I know you're not being straight with me."

Carolina did not answer.

"You weren't being straight with me, were you?"

Still Carolina did not answer.

"Am I going to stay here, or can I go home?"

"I think you can go home tomorrow or the day after at the latest."

Halleluiah turned her head and raised it slightly. "I want to die in my own home, Carolina. Not here. I want to die under my own ceiling."

"Don't talk like that, Lue."

"That's how I feel." She rested her head on the pillow again. "You have to promise me one thing though. You have to promise you won't tell Tonio that it's curtains for me. You haven't told him already, have you?"

Carolina shook her head no.

"Swear you won't tell him. Ever. As long as I know, that's enough. I'll just have to learn to be a good actress. He'll never guess." She turned her head slightly. "I've read on my own about people who have what I have. Most of them die after a year. First, there's the surgery. Then the therapy. Then a few good weeks and even months, if they're lucky. Then the setback. Then more surgery. More therapy. And it starts all over again." She paused. "I don't want to be worn down like that."

"It may be necessary, Lue. We might have to operate again to get what we didn't get the fist time. I'm not saying we will. I'm just saying we might."

"And if I won't let you."

Carolina did not answer.

"See," said Halleluiah. "You mean well, sweetheart. I know that. But if I'm on my way downhill, I don't want you to do anything that would keep me going for the same result anyway, give or take a few months. That would just be a slow death. I can't go that route, Carolina. I'd lose my mind, honest to Pete."

"Well, we don't have to make decisions like that now."

"It's already made. If I have to go, I want to go while I'm still myself. I don't know if I'll have the courage to stick to my guns, but I'm going to try." She closed her eyes. "As long as Tonio doesn't know, I'll bring it off somehow." After a moment she opened her eyes fully. "Carolina, I'm a happy woman. I'm really a happy woman—one in a zillion. I've been given what I've always looked for, what most women look for. I'm married to someone who loves me for just what I am—the real me, the inside-me. No deceptions, no alternatives, no plans, nothing like that. Just plain me. Once you're on the receiving end of that kind of love, you know you've had it all. It makes you think that this is why we're on this earth. There's nothing more I want, nothing else, except maybe to have this go on until I'm an old woman. But what difference do the years make? It will just be more of what I already know now. It doesn't have anything to do with years. It's now and forever at the same time, do you know what I mean? And if it's forever, then the years don't matter. Everybody wants years. But the main thing is to appreciate right now. It's like looking at Tonio right in the eyes, or looking at a baby, or a diamond. Everything else turns into nothing..."

"Lue, why..."

"No, let me get it all out. When I talk, things get clearer for me. I told you a long time ago I'm a non-stop talker. I'm even amazing myself with what's coming out of me. I sound like some kind of philosopher, right? Isn't that a laugh? Halleluiah Vargas—philosopher."

"You really should sleep. The nurse gave you something to help. I think it's the best thing for you now."

"I know. It's everything I can do right now to keep from slipping off. I'm half way there. I'm not asleep, but I'm not awake either. Maybe there's a word for that."

"Are you in any pain?"

"No, nothing. And I can move my left hand and my left foot. Look."

"Good."

"Will you do something for me?"

"Anything, Lue."

"Will you hold my hand?"

Carolina reached and took Halleluiah's right hand and squeezed it in both of hers.

"You have the softest hands," said Halleluiah. "It must be a Mexican trait. Mr. Vargas' hands are soft like that. And so are Tonio's." She waited. "I can feel your ring. Is it the one I like?"

"The same one. I bought in in Taxco. They have the best silversmiths there."

"I can feel that little bow on the top of it."

"It's the symbol of infinity."

"That's the same as forever, isn't it?"

"Close." Carolina looked at Halleluiah until their eyes met. "Let me give it to you. It would mean more to me for you to wear it. Honestly."

"I couldn't."

"Sure, you could. I'm offering it."

Halleluiah turned her eyes away. "I'll tell you what. Next year if I'm still here, I'll accept it. I'll even remind you. How's that?"

"Whatever you want. It's yours from now on as far as I'm concerned."

"Thanks, Carolina. You're so sweet to me, so good. I don't know where I'd be without you." She closed her eyes again. "Remember what you promised me though. Don't tell Tonio. Ever. Promise me that."

I CAN write again, thank God and amen. I didn't know if my head and hand would ever work together again, but they've come back. It's like I said before, Carolina. Sometimes my body is me, and sometimes it takes off on its own. I really can't trust it anymore. I never know when it's going to turn on me like a pet that gets mean all of a sudden for no good reason.

Speaking of pets, my cardinal has come back. Every morning before I went to the hospital, he used to come to the kitchen window for a handout. I got into the habit of leaving seeds for him, so he kept coming back. This morning he was back again. He looks like a little king when he perches there. And then after a few minutes Mrs. Cardinal came, and they both started picking at the seeds together. There was plenty for both of them, so there was no fighting. She's so much duller than he is. Where he's red, she's light brown. They have the same crest, but somehow he looks more dignified. It's all in how he carries himself. Can you say that about a bird? Dignified? Well, he does. More dignified than his wife.. Tonio told me that cardinals mate for life. Isn't it nice to think of that?

Like I said, today my body's my friend again. At least so far it is. Tonio watches me like an eagle, but I try to be casual. I can see that he's afraid for me, but I don't think he suspects. I'm sure of one thing. He doesn't know what you and I know. So far, I've been a pretty good actress, and you and I have a promise, remember? Besides, what good would it do if he knew?

When I left the hospital, you told me to be ready for anything, and I have been. For a week I was as good as ever. Muz and Mr. Vargas came to see me one night, and that was nice. But Tonio insisted on staying home with me. There was no summer school, and he had the time coming anyway. I navigated. I cooked. I read. He took me for a drive to his father's, and Mr. Vargas made some gazpacho because he knows how much I like his gazpacho. We relaxed and acted as if nothing had happened. It was just a perfect evening. Just family, and I like that better than anything in the world. If I had a family spirit like that when I was growing up, maybe I wouldn't talk my head off all the time. Talk, talk, talk. I don't know how Tonio stands me. Sometimes I can't even stand myself. But talking out whatever I'm thinking helps me make sense of things. I don't make sense all the time, but sometimes I do make sense. At least I try.

I was doing terrific until last week. On Monday I started to feel some numbness in my writing hand. Then it went away. but at the same time I started to feel sick—stomach-sick. I threw up. I kept telling Tonio that maybe I had the flu. But inside I was scared. In fact, I'm still scared. Not as scared as I was then, but scared enough. The pen is shaking right now in my hand because I'm thinking about it.

The next morning I couldn't get out of bed. My hands and feet were numb, and it took me forever and a day to say a single word. Tonio called you, and you told him to drive me to the hospital. Meanwhile, I kept trying to get up, but my feet wouldn't hold me. Tonio held me in his arms and kept me calm. And I started to improve. My voice came back to me. I—you guessed it—I started to cry. I don't know now if I was crying out of fear or disappointment. But it wasn't out of pain. I didn't have any pain at all. When I calmed down, I told Tonio, "I don't want to go back to the hospital. If I get better, I get better. If I'm going to die, I want to die in my own house." Tonio told me to stop talking about dying, but I made him promise not to take me back to the hospital no matter what. And he promised. He said he wouldn't take me anywhere I didn't want to go. Then we just waited. The numbness went away for a minute, then it came back. Away and back. I told Tonio I had to go to the bathroom. I knew I couldn't take care of myself. Tonio just picked me up and carried me into the bathroom and helped me in there. Helped me? He did it all for me. And he was as good as a man can be about it. He changed me and cleaned me, and what else can I say? I couldn't think of anyone else in the world who would do that for me or who I would let do that for me, even Muz, but Tonio did. Then he washed me and dried me and helped me into a fresh pair of pajamas. He never left me for a second that whole day. Then when the numbness finally went away, he left me just long enough to make me some soup. And I was able to keep that down.

I was just like a baby to him that day, somebody to take total care of. And I felt such a love for him through all that time that I would have... I don't know what I would have done, but I would have done something. You feel like you want nothing, just him. You want to turn into him, if that makes sense. You realize that you're loved from top to bottom, loved when you're at your worst, loved when you can't really love back in a way that matters. I never felt so helpless and yet so valuable in my whole life.

But I still know that what happened wasn't a good sign. All that you couldn't or wouldn't tell me kept coming back to me, and I started to think that this was the beginning of the end, that I would just get more and more helpless until one day when it would be all over. And I prayed that that wouldn't happen. Not for a while. I prayed myself to sleep, and when I woke, it was dark, and Tonio was asleep in the chair next to the bed, and my legs and hands were as good as new again. I whispered to Tonio, and he was up in a flash. I showed him how I could move my hands and feet, and I told him to get into bed, and he did and we put our arms around one another like two people trying to keep one another warm in a blizzard, and we slept that way.

That was a week ago, and so far I haven't had any recurrences, which isn't bad for a so far two-time loser. I'm back to taking every day as it comes. This is the first time I've tried to write, and my handwriting hasn't changed, so I guess that says something too.

Today was Tonio's first day back to school. There's nothing in session now, but he just wanted to go back and check on the instruments and any telephone messages. I could see he was worrying about school and me at the same time, so I shoo-ed him out the door and told him I was a big girl now. So, I'm alone for a while. He said we'd have some cappuccino when he got back and then just sit on the couch together and watch the sun set.

There's my cardinal again, and Mrs. Cardinal is right beside him. They're pecking at the seeds I left for them. Each one has a share, and they don't fight about it. Isn't it something about birds? They live. They fly. They eat. They make their nests. They mate. And then one day they die. It just happens. They don't know in advance that it's going to happen. It's just another phase for them. They seem to go from day to day. I'll bet they don't remember much. And they don't think ahead. They live from now to now to now until it just stops.

Sure, I think about dying, Carolina. But there's nothing really to face. You don't know anything you didn't know before, just that death has a schedule in place now. But that doesn't make you think any differently. I used to think that most people die like campfires—just burning down to a final piece of ash. But only a minority go that way, right? Most people go while they have a lot of living still left in them. All it takes is one thing—one small thing sometimes—to cut them down. Slow. Or fast. Which is better? I don't know, really.

I vote for the birds. They get taken out just like that. They have no idea that it's coming. They're spared thinking about it in advance. So as far as they're concerned, they act as if they're going to live forever. And that's good enough for them. And for me.

MOST of the faces in the church were Mexican, as he expected, but there were others. The only face he recognized instantly was Tonio's father's. The old man was sitting in the second pew, his cane hooked over the pew in front of him. The sight of him immediately transported Father Sanchez back to Laredo when he was a boy accompanying his mother to Mass on the second of November. After the death of his wife, Mr. Vargas was always there, and Tonio was always with him.

After Father Sanchez finished reading the gospel to the congregation, he closed the red leather-bound testament softly and put it on a shelf under the speaker's platform.

"Hermanos y hermanas," he began. He proceeded to speak in Spanish, explaining the meaning of the feast of the day to people who, he was sure, were aware of its meaning from the time they were weaned. He did not go into detail by tracing the feast back to the Mayans, the visits to gravesites with marigolds and food, the Indian belief that the souls of the dead were never remote but always near those left alive, particularly on the first and second of November.

When he finished speaking in Spanish, he repeated his sermon in English, this time filling in the details that seemed superfluous before. He noticed that his remarks had a disquieting effect on several people, so he concluded his sermon by saying, "Many people believe that this custom among the Mexican people is a morbid preoccupation, but it is really an act of love. For the Mexican, death is a misfortune that kills everything but memory. The result is that memory becomes the treasure-chest of love. Remembering the dead is how those left alive continue to love them. That is why Mexican people light special candles on this day and exchange gifts and prepare special foods. They keep a place at their tables for those who are gone, and they even prepare the missing person's favorite dish." He smiled, but the only ones in the congregation who returned his smile were the Mexicans. "These tangible things, these candles, these flowers and gifts and foods make death less awesome. It becomes a familiar part of life, a domestic part of life. Let me conclude by quoting one of Mexico's greatest poets on El Día de los Muertos—the Day of the Dead: 'The Mexican... is familiar with death...jokes about it, caresses it, sleeps with it, celebrates it: it is one of his favorite toys and his most steadfast love.'"

After he finished saying Mass and changing his vestments, Father Sanchez reviewed his agenda for the day. First, the hospital calls. then visits to three members of the parish who were housebound. Then his regular visit to the prison in the afternoon. After that he would have time to see Tonio.

A few moments later, as he was backing his gray Escort out of the driveway, he saw Tonio's father angling his way across the parking lot. Despite his unsteadiness, the old man still maintained a certain dignity as he moved. It was the dignity that Father Sanchez associated with the blind—a definite sense of who they were no matter where they were. They conveyed it without even trying. It was true as a reflex.

He suddenly remembered how Lue had described him. "Tonio's father is so quiet, so deep. He has that Mexican way of looking at the world, and you get the feeling that he sees it all—life, death, birth, love, sorrow, jealousy, fairness, everything. He's always serious and quiet, but his eyes talk. And they talk in the same quiet, Mexican way. A look here, a look there, and you get the message. I know he loves me. Loves me like his own. He'd do anything for me. I wouldn't even have to ask him. He'd just know. But as long as Tonio's around, he holds back. He doesn't want to interfere. So, he just sits and looks. He answers me when I talk to him in Spanish, but he doesn't initiate anything. He gives me the feeling that he keeps a different kind of time than other people. We keep time by minutes and hours. He makes me feel that he keeps time by centuries."

AFTER Tonio's father returned from Mass, he sat in the rocker on his front porch for almost half an hour. Once he stood, made his way into the house for a glass of water and returned. Even for the short walk into the house he used his cane as much for support as balance. He took short steps. Anyone watching him would have been reminded of the measured walk of a hobbled prisoner. Once he was re-seated in the rocker, he kept up a slow rhythm until the strain of his trek to Mass left his face completely. All that remained was a vein at his temple that seemed more obvious than usual. A breeze from the sea ruffled his gray-flecked black hair and gradually dried the perspiration on his forehead. By then he was rocking so slightly that he barely seemed to be rocking at all.

Finally, he stood, leaning heavily on his cane as he did, and short-stepped his way back into the house. Once in the house he moved with a new alacrity. He leaned his cane in a corner near the door, hurried into the kitchen and returned with two votive candles, each in a differently colored saucer holder, one blue, one white. He placed them on the windowsill in the living room but slid them apart until they were separated by almost ten inches. Then he struck a kitchen match on the underside of the sill and lighted the wick of each candle as carefully and reverently as he would have done on an altar. When they were both lighted, he stepped back and watched the matching flame.

By the time Tonio reached his father's house, the two candles in the window were guttering. He saw his father in the rocker on the porch, and he felt his father's sure and even gaze follow him from the time he left his car until he was standing beside him. He kissed his father on the top of his head, then sat down on the porch step. His father continued to rock and look at him.

"I have the gazpacho in the kitchen," his father said.

Tonio smiled. "I knew you'd do that, but you didn't have to."

"In the kitchen," his father repeated.

Tonio stood and entered the house. The gazpacho was in an old mayonnaise jar on the kitchen table. He picked up the jar, re-tightened the lid and returned to the porch where his father was standing by the rocker and resting on one of its arms for support.

"Do you want to come with me?" Tonio asked.

"I want to, but I am tired, Tonio. Cansado. Muy cansado. I walked to the Mass. It was too far for me."

"I won't be long. When I get back, we'll spend the whole evening together."

"Good."

Tonio kissed the old man on the lips and went to his car. After propping the mayonnaise jar on the seat beside him so that it wouldn't tip, he drove off toward Anaheim.

All the way to Anaheim, Tonio played the concerts of Mexican songs that he and Halleluiah had listened to when he drove her home after they first met. He tried to sing along with two of the songs but discovered to his surprise that he had forgotten the words.

By the time he reached Anaheim it was already mid-afternoon. He parked in his usual spot, took the bottle of gazpacho and a bouquet of white roses that were wrapped loosely in green tissue paper. Then he headed for the slope.

Father Sanchez was already there. He did not see Tonio approaching and seemed startled when Tonio's shadow slanted across the grass in front of him.

"Paco," said Tonio. "How did you know I'd be here?"

"I didn't know. I just came. I've been busy all day. This is the only time I could come."

Tonio saw that the priest was holding a bouquet of roses, also white and sleeved in green foil.

"How are you, Tonio?" asked the priest.

Tonio shrugged. He turned away as if he did not want to meet the priest's eyes at that moment. Then he knelt down without a word, crossed himself quickly and was alone with his thoughts. The priest put his hand on Tonio's shoulder for a moment, then stepped away.

After Tonio finished and stood up, the two men looked down at the grave and headstone as if they were looking at regret itself. Then Tonio took the bouquet from Father Sanchez and, joining it with his own, propped the doubled bouquet against the headstone. Then he took the bottle of gazpacho and settled it in front of the bouquet.

"The jar has gazpacho in it. Lue loved the way my father made it, so he wanted me to bring it as something for her from him."

Father Sanchez seated himself on the grass above the headstone. Tonio sat beside him. Then he lay back on the grass, joined his hands behind his neck and looked up at the sky where the clouds were as full and white as lather and absolutely still.

"When I lie here and look up like this, I'm exactly where I want to be, Paco. I'm sad. I admit it to you. I'm so sad sometimes that I think I'm going to burst out of my skin. But after that passes, I'm all right."

"It's a beautiful spot."

Tonio sat up. He locked his arms around his raised knees. Then he leaned his forehead against the tops of his knees. Father Sanchez saw the sobs before he heard them.

"You were the best husband, Tonio," Father Sanchez said, almost on a whisper. "She told me she drew all her strength from you."

Tonio released his knees and leaned back on his arms. The tears had changed his face, softened it, giving it a kind of authenticity that only sorrow could earn for it. "She was no burden for me. I knew for months that she wasn't going to make it."

"Carolina told you?"

"No. But she didn't have to. I could see it in her face. But I made her promise not to tell Lue, so Lue never really did know. She thought all the time that she would live through it. She always had hope in her life. You know what she would tell me?"

"No. Dígame."

"She would tell me that the best way to live is to believe you'll live forever. She used to say that birds think they'll live forever because they don't know they'll die." He turned on his back again and joined his hands on his chest. "We were having coffee. She always liked the way I made coffee. And I said that we ought to watch the sun set because it would never set just that way again. And that's when she died. She died looking at the sunset. No, she didn't die. That's not the word. She left. She just left while I was talking to her. It was as if she went to sleep right in the middle of a word. It happened that quickly."

The priest watched him. He knew that Tonio was saying what he had to say, and he made no attempt to reply.

"I miss her, Paco." He closed his eyes and lay perfectly still. "I love her now the way you love someone who's gone. It's the worst pain, but somehow she's closer to me even though she's gone." He paused. "I never thought I'd be telling anyone this. This day was always something outside of me. Now it's inside. I'm part of it." He opened his eyes. The tears were sliding out to the corners of both eyes. "I remember once I was in Monterey, and there was a funeral. It was a funeral for a little boy. And there was a band playing happy music. And the little boy's brother was in the band. He was playing the trumpet, playing that happy music, and the tears were running down his cheeks, because—heaven or no heaven—it was his brother."

Father Sanchez looked at his watch. "I have to leave, Tonio. I need to make one more house call before dinner."

"I'm all right now. I'll go with you. Just give me one more minute, please." He looked up at the sky. "See. The clouds have started to move. That's a sign."

Father Sanchez stood and brushed the seat of his pants to get rid of the grass cuttings there. For the first time he really studied the headstone—a square slab the size of a small window with HALLELUIAH cut into it and centered. That was all.

"You don't have dates on the stone, Tonio."

Tonio stood up and looked at the priest. It was as if he had been anticipating the question.

"You know, Paco, Lue didn't change at all during that one year we had together. She never let that awful thing turn her into anything but what she was. She stayed herself. All the time."

"I was talking about the stone. They forgot the dates."

"They didn't forget. I told them. No dates. How can you put dates on forever? You're a priest, Paco. I shouldn't have to be the one to tell you that."

After shaking hands, they went to their cars and quickly drove off. Neither of them glimpsed Carolina who had parked at the far end of the cemetery's parking lot. She had been watching them both but had remained in her car. She had huddled down so that they would not see her. She did not want to have to explain herself.

Once both cars were gone, Carolina left her car and walked slowly to Halleluiah's grave. She walked without deviation, her eyes on the rising ground she was covering with long, sure strides.

When she reached the grave, she knelt down, blessed herself and closed her eyes. After she finished, she remained on her knees. She re-arranged the double bouquet of white roses so that each flower had more room to breathe. She could not understand the presence of the filled mayonnaise jar, but she did not disturb it. She looked at the name on the gravestone, saying it silently as her eyes scanned the letters.

She sat back on her ankles and opened her purse and removed a small metal nail file. Then, setting her purse aside, she dug a hole in the earth beside the flowers. When she finished, she wiped the file on the grass and put it back in her purse. The hole was barely the thickness of her thumb and less than three inches deep.

Then Carolina eased a silver ring from the little finger of her left hand. She held it in her palm for a moment longer, feeling the small bow of silver against the skin of her thumb. Then she dropped it into the hole she had dug and filled in the hole quickly. She looked at her watch. It had not taken her as long as she thought it would. She still had an extra half hour before she had to be back at the hospital. She sat back on the grass. The sky was a complete circus of clouds. In an hour the sun would be down, but now there was only the slanting light of the late afternoon that made everything seem peaceful and complete.

SAMUEL HAZO

The author of books of poetry, fiction, essays and plays, Samuel Hazo is the founder and director of the International Poetry Forum in Pittsburgh, Pennsylvania. He is also McAnulty Distinguished Professor of English Emeritus at Duquesne University, where he taught for forty-three years. From 1950 until 1957 he served in the United States Marine Corps (Regular and Reserve), completing his tour as a captain. He earned his Bachelor of Arts degree magna cum laude from the University of Notre Dame, a Master of Arts degree from Duquesne University and his doctorate from the University of Pittsburgh. Some of his previous works are THE LESS SAID, THE TRUER, THE NEXT TIME WE SAW PARIS, AND THE TIME IS, LIKE A MAN GONE MAD and SEXES: THE MARRIAGE DIALOGUES (Poetry), THE TIME REMAINING and IF NOBODY CALLS, I'M NOT HOME (Fiction), TELL IT TO THE MARINES (Drama), THE STROKE OF A PEN and OUTSPOKENLY YOURS (Essays), SMITHEREENED APART (Critique of the poetry of Hart Crane), THE PITTSBURGH THAT STAYS WITHIN YOU (Memoir awarded the 2018 IPPY national bronze citation for creative non-fiction) and THE WORLD WITHIN THE WORD: MARITAIN AND THE POET (Critique). His translations include Denis de Rougemont's THE GROWL OF DEEPER WATERS, Nadia Tueni's LEBANON: TWENTY POEMS FOR ONE LOVE and Adonis' THE PAGES OF DAY AND NIGHT. In 2003 a selective collection of his poems, JUST ONCE, received the Maurice English Poetry Award. He has been awarded twelve honorary doctorates. He was honored with the Griffin Award for Creative Writing from the University of Notre Dame, his alma mater, and was chosen to receive his tenth honorary doctorate from the university in 2008. A National Book Award finalist, he was named Pennsylvania's first State Poet by Governor Robert Casey in 1993, and he served until 2003.

Made in the USA
Middletown, DE
10 February 2023